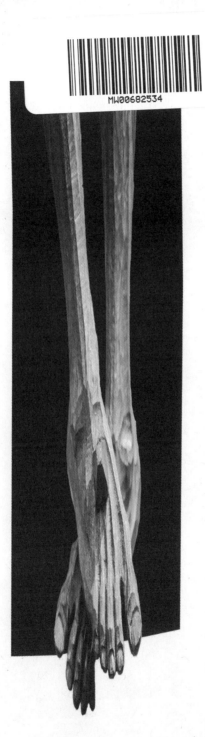

THE OBESE CHRIST

Also by Larry Tremblay

NOVELS
The Bicycle Eater *
Piercing *

PLAYS
Abraham Lincoln Goes to the Theatre *
Blues Hands
Talking Bodies: Four Plays
    (including *A Trick of Fate, Anatomy Lesson,*
    The Dragonfly of Chicoutimi, and *Ogre*) *
The Ventriloquist *
War Cantata *

* Published by Talonbooks

THE OBESE CHRIST

A NOVEL BY

LARRY TREMBLAY

TRANSLATED BY SHEILA FISCHMAN

TALONBOOKS

Original title: Le Christ obèse
© 2012 Éditions Alto et Larry Tremblay
Translation © 2014 Sheila Fischman

Talonbooks
278 East 1st Avenue, Vancouver, British Columbia, Canada V5T 1A6
www.talonbooks.com

First printing: 2014

Typeset in Arno
Printed and bound in Canada on 100% post-consumer recycled paper

Interior and cover design by Typesmith
Cover photograph: Shutterstock 98961095 (member: Dieter H)

Talonbooks gratefully acknowledges the financial support of the Canada
Council for the Arts, the Government of Canada through the Canada Book
Fund, and the Province of British Columbia through the British Columbia
Arts Council and the Book Publishing Tax Credit.

This work was originally published in French as *Le Christ obèse* by Éditions
Alto, Quebec City, Quebec, in 2012. We acknowledge the financial support
of the Government of Canada, through the National Translation Program,
for our translation activities.

Library and Archives Canada Cataloguing in Publication

Tremblay, Larry, 1954–
[Christ obèse. English]
    The obese Christ / Larry Tremblay ; translated by Sheila Fischman.

Translation of: Le Christ obèse.
Issued in print and electronic formats.
ISBN 978-0-88922-842-9 (pbk.).—ISBN 978-0-88922-843-6 (epub)

    I. Fischman, Sheila, translator II. Title. III. Title: Christ obèse.
English.

PS8589.R445C4713 2014   C843'.54   C2014-901526-7
                                                  C2014-901527-5

For Claude Poissant

The urge to pray has nothing to do with faith.

— CIORAN

THE THING

The arrow was about to pierce the nape of my neck.
Though I ran as fast as I could, raced down steep roads,
leapt across ditches, climbed hills, it anticipated my every
move, pursued me like a baying hound. I had no chance
to escape. Resigned, I stopped running, and stiff and
straight as a tree, awaited the fatal blow.

A sharp, snapping sound saved me.

It took a few moments before I realized I'd dozed off
on my mother's grave. I had been asleep for a long time.
The cemetery was now plunged into night. Rain fell gently,
rain warmer than the surrounding air. I was no longer
alone, I could hear shouting nearby. Intrigued, I slipped
like a shadow through graves and groves until I reached
a small mound. From there I could see a group of men.
They were laughing and shouting words that I couldn't
make out. Their hazy silhouettes stood out in the bluish
light of the moon. Four men in their twenties or maybe
younger. They were bending over something and kicking
it. Had they extricated themselves from a grave like the
Four Horsemen of the Apocalypse?

I approached them to get a better look. They wore
uniforms and peaked caps. Their laughs became less
frequent, then were swallowed by a disturbing silence.
One of the four men brought a bottle to his lips. He
drank, then tossed the bottle in my direction. Thinking
he'd seen me, I got out of there fast, crawling like an

animal until my knees were scraped raw, a victim of uncontrollable panic. Shaking, teeth chattering, strength gone, I collapsed near my mother's grave, not daring to move. I waited one long moment. The rain had stopped. A light mist drifted in the air. The breath of the dead escaped from the ground, stinking and cold.

I pricked up my ears. Nothing. All I heard was the rustling of the elm trees that circled part of the cemetery. My fear assuaged, I returned to the place where I'd spotted the four men. They were gone. Now I knew for sure: the one who'd thrown the bottle just wanted to get rid of it. It was strictly coincidental that he'd thrown it in my direction. I approached the thing they'd been kicking with their boots. It was a young girl. A young girl who must have been beautiful. Even in this painful situation I couldn't help noticing her fine features, realizing that she must have been lovely before.

Now her face was bloody. Lifting her, I noticed a long branch sticking out from under her dress. I pulled on it, threw it in the air with all my might. The poor girl had suffered the very worst abuse.

I ran from the cemetery, the young girl in my arms, afraid the Four Horsemen of the Apocalypse would burst out of the darkness and make me in turn suffer torments too shameful to mention. It was only when I saw the entrance with its tall wrought-iron gate that I could finally catch my breath. In the distance I heard the muffled sounds of the city, its moist breathing. That was enough to calm me. I headed for my car. Opened the trunk and threw the limp body inside.

I drove across the city, relieved to recognize familiar streets, illuminated signs, lighted shop windows. I must not think about the branch, must concentrate on driving, on the light from headlights, on what lay ahead of me.

With stunning confidence given the circumstances, I parked under the branches of the oak tree that hid my mother's house. It must have been past midnight. The rain had cleared the air and it was no longer muggy. I glanced around. Nobody. In the distance I could see the city lights and below, the halo of street lamps in which I could make out the suicidal flights of insects, whirlwinds of life intent on their own demise. My mother's house was the last one built on a small hill and the closest neighbours lived half a block away. I saw no one and running into anyone at this late hour would have surprised me. Few people visited the neighbourhood. I lived in isolation.

I leaned against the back end of my car, not thinking, savouring my solitude. I stood there unmoving for a long moment. Then I opened the trunk. An odour assailed me. The girl … What a disaster! Her dress, her legs, were soiled with excrement. I opened the garden gate, ran down the path until I couldn't hold it in any longer; I vomited in Mama's acacias. Panicking like a child caught misbehaving, I took shelter in the house, slammed the door behind me, went upstairs, and got into bed without bothering to undress.

THE BEAST

A simple odour shook me awake. Slowly I realized I'd had
the courage to remove that long branch from the body,
a feat of nerves and guts not accessible to everyone. The
young girl, in the grip of a spasm, had let out a feeble
moan. It was at that precise moment I knew I was not
dealing with a corpse but with a person whose life was in
danger. Suffering. My head under the pillow, on the verge
of asphyxiation, I didn't understand how I could have
stuffed her in the trunk like she was a bag of trash. I realized I really had seen her move, breathe … but then left
her for dead and ran away – simply because of the smell.

A simple smell, the one found in every human's
entrails at every second of his or her existence.

I cursed myself. I would never do anything well unless
I carried through to the end something I had started.
How could I pity that poor girl unless I accepted the
consequences of the violence she'd endured? I pushed
my pillow. Got up and peeked out my bedroom window.
The rain-wet street glistened in places. Not one lighted
window at the closest neighbours'. The people in this part
of town were sleeping peacefully. They had earned their
sleep. They rested from fatigue, from anxiety. Forgetting
their worries, their quarrels, the endless list of things large
and small they had to accomplish.

Except for her. Except for me.

Why hadn't I closed the trunk? I realized I'd been reckless, stupid. I had acted against my own will, realized I could no longer hide it from myself: if I had not raced to a hospital or a police station, if I hadn't howled for help, if I hadn't called an ambulance and roused the whole city around that dying girl, then very well. It could only be because I had decided to take care of her myself.

I would be her saviour.

I went downstairs and opened the front door. Nothing had changed. No one had alerted the police. Everything was still possible. I took a few steps down the pathway in the lane. The trunk yawned open, its jaws quite thoughtlessly agape. Rain dripped from the metal lid.

I retraced my steps back into the house, grabbed the cloth from the table in the living room where I ate, having abandoned the dining room that seemed too big now that my mother had died. I took the tablecloth and went outside. Walked to the trunk of the car. Something moved inside. Not the girl, something else. Something was scratching. I bent slowly over the trunk. A beast pounced on me. I drew back, fell over. Banged my head on the concrete sidewalk. Before I fainted, I saw, in blood-red letters, a line from Homer that I'd read in school. A line that recurred often in the *Iliad* to signify that death had just taken a soldier, piercing him with a lance or decapitating him with his opponent's two-edged sword. A very simple line that I recited like a prayer before sleep.

And the darkness descended on his eyes.

Then I collapsed.

Day had dawned by the time I regained consciousness. The sidewalk was dry and a lark was launching into song from the branches of the oak. The first thing I recognized was the tablecloth. It covered part of my body. My head ached atrociously. I dragged myself to the trunk of the car. On my knees, I took a worried look inside. She was there. It was the first time I had seen her in daylight. Her face was swollen, deformed by her assailants' blows, her red dress torn in places. Dark blood stained her arms and legs. She had just one shoe on. I wrapped her in the tablecloth as best I could. Kicked the trunk shut and carried the girl into the house. I set her down in the middle of the living room. Standing up, I felt faint. In the main-floor bathroom I splashed water on my face. Discovered a bump on my head. I also noticed a fine scratch near my left eye. A cat. No doubt about it, a cat had jumped on my face. It had been attracted by the putrid smell emanating from the trunk. I could think of no other explanation. Cats are diabolical creatures.

THE TUB

It was Sunday, one of those mornings when the world seems to have forgotten to turn. Even the wind had deserted the street. In this somniferous, suicidal neighbourhood, Sundays only accentuated the desolation of this part of town that overlooked the city with contempt. A blessing it hadn't happened on a Monday. I was sure at least no neighbour had seen me go into my house with a body wrapped in a tablecloth.

I looked at my watch: barely six o'clock. I went back to the living room and looked around. No one. I went upstairs, opened the bathroom door. It adjoined my mother's room and was much more spacious than the one on the main floor. It was home to a large claw-footed tub. A small skylight let in the daylight. I ran a bath, went down to the living room, and with great effort carried the girl up and shoved her, fully dressed, into the tub. The water immediately darkened and turned crimson. I pulled the plug, ran water to fill the tub again. I noticed one of the girl's eyelids open for a fraction of a second. I was perplexed: was I doing the right thing? Getting rid of her stains had seemed like a priority. I opened the medicine chest where my mother had kept pill bottles and the few cosmetics she had allowed herself. I'd thrown nothing out. Nine months had passed since her death and all her belongings were still in place, scoffing at her permanent absence. In the medicine chest I found a flask of bath oil that I emptied into the tub. Opening a window at the end of the corridor, I let a little fresh air into the bathroom, propping the door open with an empty flowerpot. Turning around, I saw that the girl had slid under water. I rushed to her and grabbed her by the hair to hoist her into the open air. I fell on my behind, holding a handful of hair.

It was a wig!

I gripped the edge of the bathtub. Under the water, another face gazed at me, eyes open. The young girl actually had blonde hair, cut very short. Her features, without the impressive mass of black hair, had suddenly reorganized themselves. Her eyes were a sparkling green. They seemed to stare back at me. Her lips opened slightly and three air bubbles escaped. Fascinated, I grabbed hold of her, lifted her from the tub, and laid her on the floor. Blood still seeped from her wounds. Her chest rose more visibly. I could clearly hear her breathing. An emotion until then unknown took hold of me. A shiver. Everything, absolutely everything, depended on me. I was responsible for a life.

THE TELEPHONE

Mama would have known what to do – she'd been an ER nurse. She knew how to look after the weak and the sick. She had cared ceaselessly for my own colds and fevers and anxieties. Wounds, scars, dressings held no mystery for her. Mama would have known right away what to do for the girl.

I wiped the blood from her wounds. A cut on her right thigh looked particularly deep, and a bit of flesh dangled from it. I improvised a dressing. Turned her onto her stomach. Tried to cut off her dress with scissors but the wet cloth resisted. I managed to rip it up to her lower back. I'd made no mistake at the cemetery: her underwear was torn. Bits of bark were still stuck to the bloody fabric. I went down to the kitchen, opened the fridge, and drank some milk directly from the carton. Finally, I drained it all, sat in my usual place – the chair that faced Mama's – and dissolved into tears.

I felt paralyzed. I stared at the telephone sitting on the kitchen counter. I'd always told Mama it was a bad place for a phone. Though I explained that where she had placed it, the telephone cluttered the counter, especially when we were doing the dishes, but she always did as she pleased. Also, it was not hygienic, the handset was spattered with water as soon as the tap was turned on, because the damn tap needed fixing. I was sure that a telephone should not be exposed to moisture, which could only damage it. Usually my mother didn't listen when I made this kind of remark. She was convinced that I was completely impractical. She would retort that if there was something in this house that was out of order, it was my head and the thoughts it produced. Since her death the phone had rung only on rare occasions. Not for a second had I considered moving it.

The thought of calling for help tormented me. I couldn't imagine how I could get out of it all on my own. That unknown life waiting for me upstairs on the bathroom floor, those green eyes – how could I take care of them? I already had trouble taking care of myself. To open my eyes in the morning and see that it was me, again me, who opened them and not someone else, no matter who else, even a dog, plunged my still-groggy body into a torpor that would not leave me until late afternoon. As if my soul could be roused only at the moment when the sun switched off. And now on this Sunday morning, in the tired September light falling from the kitchen window, I was confronted with this reality: a girl lay unconscious in my mother's bathroom, victim of the brutality of men.

I finally emerged from my lethargy, grabbed the telephone, unplugged it, took it to the living room, and plugged it in again. I went back upstairs. As soon as I saw through the doorway into the bathroom, I couldn't breathe. The girl was not there.

A SMALL ANIMAL

The door stood slightly ajar. I stuck my head in. Peered into my bed: was she under the covers I'd left in a tangled mess the night before? I stepped into the room. Could it be a trap? Could she have a weapon and be waiting to use it on me the moment I lifted the covers? But where would she have unearthed a weapon and why would she wish me ill? After all, I wasn't one of her assailants. I lifted the covers: no girl. Opened the clothes closet: no girl.

I exited the bedroom and let my gaze slip to the bathroom door: no trace of blood. I wanted to go to Mama's room but something caught my attention. From where I stood I could see a small animal in the bathroom. It wasn't moving. Maybe it was as frightened as I was. I had read that some animals, when they sense the presence of an enemy, stand perfectly still. I had more than once observed this questionable attempt at hiding among the squirrels that proliferate in the neighbourhood. Instead of scattering, they freeze stupidly, thinking their absence of movement makes them invisible. I took off one of my boots, tossed it into the bathroom. The small animal didn't budge. I took two more steps and exploded in laughter. What I thought was an animal was only the wig the girl had been wearing. I went to pick it up to confirm, as if I no longer trusted either my mind or my perception. Once in the bathroom, I stopped laughing. The girl was there. She had simply rolled to the wall opposite the tub.

I carried her into my mother's bedroom. To do so, I just had to nudge open the door between the bedroom and the bathroom. Mama had allowed herself the luxury of that door. To make room for it, she had sacrificed space for a shower; in its place, the workers had put in a swing door that could be pushed open from either side. This innovation had provoked a violent quarrel between my mother and me. She had got it in her head that it was essential to have a door that communicated directly with the bathroom. She totally disregarded my arguments in favour of a shower. She had declared once and for all that the bathtub was morally superior. I capitulated.

I placed the girl on the bed. For the first time, I spoke to her. I asked her name, she did not reply. I touched her, she did not react. Above Mama's bed, a crucifix had pride of place. I took it down. Opened a drawer in the chest where the bed linens were kept and hid it under a pile of sheets.

THE DRESS

I studied her body on the pink satin bedspread. Her wet dress clung to her bosom and was pulled up to the top of her thighs. I thought about sex. About what it can lead to. I was right to be wary. I'd been wary as long as I'd known it existed. I was also wary of nature. In this city buried in snow several months of the year, the arrival of spring never failed to set off vegetative histrionics. Flowers raged through the still-frozen earth and in one day flung their colours and perfumes into the face of heaven. Buds exploded on bare branches. Trees fully adorned themselves with leaves during a brief stroll. I felt stifled in the overflow of sap, in the brilliance of the too-brief, suicidal spring. I was all the more horrified in summer, the season when the libido triumphed outrageously. As soon as the temperature rose a few degrees, people dressed or rather undressed to the limit of decency and offered to as many eyes as possible their bodies made milky by winter. They would crowd onto café terraces, skin already brown, dripping with sweat, exhibiting themselves to one another like cuts of meat laid out in the sunshine. Youngest and oldest alike took part in that hormonal frenzy, a grotesque carnival where not the slightest bit of goodness, love, compassion, or genuine beauty had a chance to blossom. Given the opportunity I would have spat on the population in shorts, torn T-shirts, and skirts so short they showed their owners' pubes. I counted the days until fall. I greeted the reddening of leaves like a deliverance, their fall like a relief.

I was a November child. A month people hate. They can't stand its gravity, its destitution, its grey and sombre landscapes. They don't understand the inner beauty of the month, they have no idea.

Yes, I was born in November ... and my father died in November, on the very day of my birth. When my mother felt the first contractions she called a taxi instead of her husband, who worked in a government building in a northern suburb. She'd been angry with him all her life. Then my father was killed in his car on his way to the hospital. The delivery had been excruciating. My mother had undergone a caesarean under anaesthetic. When she awoke she was told about her husband's death, then they laid me on her chest. That was how it had happened, my mother had often repeated to me. Impossible to imagine it wasn't the truth.

My mother came into a substantial sum of money from the insurance, so the accident left her free of financial worries for a while. Then as the years passed she'd had to go back to work as a nurse, a profession she'd practised for several years before she married. Without the insurance money my mother wouldn't have been able to keep the house she and my father had purchased shortly after their marriage. Now it belonged to me, I could do whatever I wanted with it. Had I felt like it, I could have bricked over all the windows and lived in absolute darkness, far from flowers and the triumphant brightness of buds.

As it happened, I thanked heaven for that accident. I often imagined with horror what life would have been like if my father hadn't run a red light right into a movers' van that was crossing his lifeline at five that afternoon, just as the November sun was bowing out for the evening.

Mama did not remarry. No one else had slept in her bed. And so a shiver of guilt slowed my movement when I bent over to undress the girl. Dark spots already soiled the bedspread. And the scent of jasmine that still drifted, ghostly now, months after my mother's death, could not mask the stench of human misery I had just brought into her room.

I had a lot of trouble freeing the girl's arms. Her sleeves imprisoned her shoulders, which were quite broad. My awkward manoeuvres stirred no reaction in her. Lying there, deep in an unsettling immobility, she roused in me the image, ridiculous under the circumstances, of Sleeping Beauty. But that romantic relic vanished with a crash when I managed to take off her dress and her underwear. How had I failed to notice earlier that I'd brought a man back to the house?

THE CAFÉ

I fled to the street as if fire were devouring the house. But after a few steps down the sidewalk I had to turn back. I'd left without the boot I'd flung into the bathroom. Instead of going upstairs to get it and risk catching sight of the … the thing, I opened my mother's broom closet. I'd tossed my old running shoes in there one day. I pulled them on quickly and ran away, unable to control myself.

Some fifteen minutes later I'd caught my breath. I stood at an intersection, not sure where to go. The city was slowly coming to life. Church bells rang. I looked for a place where I could sit down, and caught sight of a restaurant sign. Began running in that direction. It didn't open till eleven for Sunday brunch. I kicked the glass door. The action alarmed me, it was unlike me. I walked towards a park. Took a seat on a little bench covered with dew. Summer was dying. From the ground rose a thin fog. Blood swelled my temples, awakening the pain in my head. I should have gone to the hospital. Maybe I had a concussion … I felt my bump. It was even bigger. I was going to die. Was it really a cat that had jumped in my face? Who was the man I'd just left alone in the house? What was I hoping for? That he would dissolve when left alone a few hours, that when I got home Mama's bed would be immaculate, that I would wake up soon and leave this nightmare, find myself still asleep on her grave? What had I done?

A good hour later I'd finally calmed down. Without realizing it I had started to walk again, retracing my steps. The restaurant spotted earlier was now open. I hesitated for a long moment before going in. I took a table in the corner. Some customers were already seated. I ordered the Sunday morning special: eggs, sausage, fruit, toast, and plenty of coffee. I felt famished and ate with a surprising appetite. I was extremely polite with the waitress, even good humoured. When she asked if I wanted more coffee, I said yes, adding that the coffee was excellent, which was false. The coffee was mediocre.

My meal finished, I observed people at other tables. The customers were young, many of them pairs, some with children. I was the only loner. At a nearby table a couple in their early twenties were just sitting down. She wore a summer dress. From what I could see of his broad back, he was well built. I pictured him kicking a ball on a playing field surrounded by an admiring crowd, with hundreds of girls applauding him. When the boy bent over his plate I got a better look at the luminous face of the girl, framed by black hair. Their love couldn't have been more than a week or two old, I was sure of it. I could detect à kind of passion emanating from them. I'd often observed new couples like them on the Metro or in the street. They caught your attention, as if the emotion that filled them, brand new, couldn't keep still, overflowed their bodies, permeated their clothes, making them more colourful than everyone around them. They spoke to bring their faces closer together, more intimately, and to transform their words into kisses. Their hands never stopped touching. If they moved apart it was only to touch again a few moments later with more voracity. Lovers attracted me and disgusted me.

As I paid my bill I took a last look at the couple facing me. The boy stroked the girl's cheek with astonishing delicacy. His fingers were large, his action small. Their legs touched. The girl gazed at her lover as if nothing around him existed, as if his whole life were absorbed in that caress, suspended from the tips of his heavy fingers. I suddenly felt tremendously relieved: I would never be like them. My fingertips would never stroke the cheek of a woman I love. On this sunny Sunday morning, that obvious fact touched my heart. Far from saddening me, it filled me with new strength. There was no question of behaving like an ordinary teenager.

I would never be like them because I am who I am, and no one in this restaurant would ever suspect what kind of man I am. No one would ever suspect what I'd achieved the night before. No one but me would have done what I had done. They didn't know the bald man who had eaten peacefully at a table close to theirs. They would never know that man.

I closed the restaurant door, determined to complete what I had started.

OUR FATHER

Half an hour later I was back in my own neighbourhood. As soon as I spotted my car in the shadow of the enormous oak I slowed down, trying to appear normal. A woman walked by, pushing her baby in a stroller. She seemed anxious, perhaps her child was sick? Should I smile at her? I let her pass by before I went back to my car. I bent discreetly over the closed trunk and sniffed. It gave off an acrid smell. I would have to clean it before the stench of shit filled the car. I went into the house, picked up the tablecloth in which I had wrapped the body of the phony girl. It was terribly dirty. I rolled it into a ball, stuffed it into a plastic bag, and threw it in the garbage. I went back to the living room to see if the cloth had soiled the carpet, which was from Kashmir. My paternal grandfather had brought it back from a trip to India. I got down on all fours to examine it. Two spots. The rug was valuable and the sole legacy my father had received from his father. My mother had inherited it. It had always been in our living room. Many stories more false than true had been told about the rug, especially about its first owner. My grandfather had lived in Himalayan caves, survived a cobra bite, and had even joined in a tiger hunt. His carpet told me of a world different from mine. As a child I'd spent hours musing over its arabesques, intertwined drawings in which one day I would recognize a hunting scene, the next day a jungle full of dangers or the secret map of a mysterious world. I would have to wrench myself away from the living room, leaving the sadness of my childhood on the flying carpet.

I came back from the kitchen with a damp cloth and rubbed the two spots. The dried blood became a little paler but not enough. I went to look for the little brush my mother used for scrubbing pots and pans. By scrubbing I managed to make the spots disappear completely. I cleaned the brush with tap water and dish soap, then went upstairs. On my way up I could hear my heartbeat. I'd thought I would fool it by putting off the moment when I would go back upstairs. But the heart is an anxious animal, always on guard, worse than a paranoid dog.

First, I went into the bathroom. The water in the tub had taken on a disgusting colour. I would have to clean it as soon as possible. I looked at myself in the mirror. Examined the scratch near my eye, it had to be a cat or if not, what? I waved at myself. Said hello, asked how I was. Replied that I was well, that all would be well, that I was a grown man, a decisive man. My grief had expired, the memory of my mother was fading.

I pushed open the door adjoining Mama's bedroom.

The ... boy hadn't moved. His mouth gaped open, his breathing was erratic. The red dress was flung to the foot of the bed, like a pile of dirty rags. I took the garment down to the kitchen and tossed it into a plastic bag. I had a good supply. My mother had insisted on keeping them. She didn't like throwing things out. The house was crammed full of empty jars, all kinds of bottles, cans. She had neatly folded grocery bags so she could store them in a cardboard box stowed under the sink.

I went into the backyard, tossed the bag into the garbage can, then went back up to the bedroom with a damp towel. I moistened the boy's lips, mopped his brow. I noticed for the first time a large wound on his head. It wasn't bleeding. A thick scab had already formed. He had no doubt received a violent kick in that place. His fingers were scraped. Some nails were broken, still black with earth. One was bent back. He must have crawled with the strength born of despair to escape his assailants. As for me, I could neither close my eyes nor run away again: the task seemed enormous.

I sat down beside him, gazing at him. Never had I heard such silence in this room. I knew very little about silence. In fact the only silence I knew was my mother's, her way of imposing her will on mine, of forcing me to nip in the bud the ideas that jostled each other behind my brow. Something was going on in that silence and it tortured me. Never had I dared to make the sound of my fear audible over her silence.

Ever since the young man had been in the bedroom I had felt I shared a silence still too young to describe, a silence that covered with a shudder the dust motes hanging in a ray of sunlight that slanted through the window. I whispered one Our Father, then another.

It was my mother who insisted I learn that prayer by heart. Just as she had been adamant that I go with her to Mass. I'd been mad at her for forcing me to behave like a pious child till I entered my teens. Back then who but me could recite a prayer by heart? I'd never been able to feel that I was like others. Only one thing really excited me: pain. I cut myself. I did it on the sly. To cover the scars, I always wore trousers and long-sleeved shirts. During the heat of summer my mother would call me crazy. She would have liked me to go wild in one of those public pools where kids my age urinated in their bathing suits, swam in their shared grime. One day, I pushed my morbid fascination further: I slit my wrists. My mother found me unconscious when she came home from work. I'd wakened up in the hospital where she worked. The shame: it was the first thing I felt when I regained consciousness. Feeling as if I were naked in front of a crowd of strangers. My mother had rushed into my room, pulled back the sheets to check the doctor hadn't misled her. He had just told her about the scars all over my body. She slapped me, then she collapsed in tears. I promised not to do it again.

A priest came to see me during my time in the hospital. An elderly man with sparse, dirty grey hair. He was missing some teeth, which disgusted me. He sat in a chair placed at an angle to my bed, breathing loudly. He asked if he could say a prayer for me. I could smell his putrid breath. I had not replied and closed my eyes to make him disappear. He was some kind of chaplain who reeled through the wards in search of souls on the verge of expiring, of leaving their bodies. His appearance next to a patient must arouse the fear of death, even provoke it sooner. I had no intention of dying in a hospital bed amid the smell of disinfectant. If I did want to die, I would do it where I wanted, when I wanted. I kept mulling over these thoughts in my head when the first words came to me. The priest was still there and his stinking mouth began to mumble an Our Father. I kept my eyes shut. More and more tense in my bed, I imagined that the words of the prayer were loaded with filth, weighed down by deadly disease. I wouldn't have been surprised, on opening my eyes, to catch a glimpse at the foot of my bed of a mass of grey shells sticky with slime, small corpses of words fallen from the priest's mouth. He did it again with a second Our Father, then a third. I could have called for help, yelled at him to leave me alone, but something in me – a stiffness within my muscles – let go. As if water were running down my spine. When I opened my eyes the priest had gone.

Our Father who art in heaven, hallowed be thy name …

I knew those words. They concealed no shade of meaning, no power of evocation. But here in this hospital bed, they had started to sparkle.

THE AMBULANCE

My mother was small in stature, bony, with conspicuous veins on her arms. She walked quickly and always seemed to be late. She breathed erratically, like an animal on the lookout. She did not look happy. She was an exemplary nurse however and patients liked her. I'd learned all that when she herself was a patient in the same hospital where she had worked. At each of my visits someone never failed to remind me that my mother was important. In addition to a thirty-year-long career, she had never made a single mistake, never complained. She was even considered to be a cheerful woman who occasionally told jokes. How could someone enjoy taking care of intubated patients, the permanent smell of medicines and bodies adrift, tolerate the yellowish light from ceiling lights that were always on, breathe the corrupted air of the gigantic hospitals that the evening news declared were unhealthy? My mother was a saint.

I should have admired her courage, told her that I, her son, couldn't have accomplished a tenth of what she'd had to do to support us both. Never had I told her that she was an exemplary woman, a woman who'd sacrificed herself, loved by the beings she had taken care of so lightheartedly, a quality she'd always kept hidden from me. For my mother had only one face for me, the face of a sad and dreary woman, despite the vitality of her body.

Her appearance had changed drastically during the months when she'd been cared for at home. Her skin took on a different colour. Her legs became swollen, the rest of her body was diminished, her eyes seemed to swallow her face. Towards the end she couldn't get up to go to the bathroom. I bought diapers. I had to do it several times, at first bothered so much by the sales clerks' looks that I could feel beads of sweat in my armpits. But a person can get used to anything, particularly to that which inspires horror and disgust, and I finally realized the diapers were innocuous, necessary, useful. My mother needed them. They were available for purchase because shops had found that people would buy them. Any idiot would have understood that the diapers would be increasingly in demand, given the aging population. I was convinced that the world had a purpose, that God wanted it, and that these diapers were a harbinger.

Putting a diaper on the young man was easier than I'd imagined. In the bathroom, I took a towel my mother had received from a patient, a beach towel with a dragonfly embroidered by the patient herself. It was, then, according to my mother's evaluation, an odd gift. It was also the first and last gift she'd received from a patient. She had never used the towel, reserving it for some special occasion that had never arisen. I covered the young man with the towel.

I went down to make myself a coffee, then waited till evening, sitting motionless. Around eleven o'clock I opened the front door. The street was deserted. I heard electricity crackling through the street lamps. I spotted some windows still lit up. No solitary walker or pair of lovers looking for a secret place. I opened the trunk of my car, inspected it briefly, then went into the house.

I returned with a bucket filled with Javex. Equipped with rubber gloves, I cleaned the trunk. Then poured the gloves and the contents of the bucket down a manhole in the street near the car. I went inside, climbed upstairs, picked up the wig from the bathroom floor, stuffed it into a plastic bag, and went out to the backyard to throw it in the garbage. Then all at once I changed my mind and went back up to stow it in my mother's dresser. As I was closing the drawer I sensed a gaze running over my back like an insect. I turned around abruptly. The young man was sleeping or in a coma, I wasn't sure which.

I observed him. For the first time I wondered seriously about the state of his health. Maybe I should have slapped him, just to jolt him out of his lethargy? But I wasn't sure about that approach, invented no doubt by scriptwriters. My mother would never have allowed me to slap an unconscious patient to revive him.

How could I feed a person in his condition? For that matter, just what was his condition? What sort of care did he need? If he died, what would I do with him? With his body? And if he survived?

Before all those questions paralyzed me, I pushed open the door next to the bathroom and spent a good hour cleaning the tub of its rings of grime. Then I drew myself a hot bath. Drained by everything I'd just lived through during the past twenty-four hours, I closed my eyes and slipped gradually into a dream in which, again, I was pursued by an arrow. Panicking, I ran through a swampy forest. It became harder and harder to move, as my boots sank deep into the mud. I couldn't free myself, a prisoner of the muck. I shrieked for help. A woman tried to assist me, but she was too late. Disgusted as if I'd just soaked in water the young man had soiled, I shot out of the bath. I towelled myself, went to my room, put on the flannel pyjamas I wore when the thermometer dipped below zero, and wrapped myself in blankets, enjoying the fluffy softness of the cloth against my skin.

But I couldn't sleep. I was still haunted by my dream. The woman who came to my aid reminded me of the nurse who'd cared for my mother before she was hospitalized. As soon as I'd seen her I had felt something like affection for her. Josiane Gravel wasn't beautiful. In those days I had watched her surreptitiously, trying to understand what made her ugly, as that was the impression that struck you on seeing her for the first time. At least that is what I'd told myself, though I knew full well that there must exist in this city a person who would say that this woman, though not beautiful, was however pleasant. Her ugliness was in fact reassuring and I had no trouble imagining that I could have loved Josiane Gravel, it would have taken just a little effort.

For the first time in my life I had glimpsed the possibility of approaching a woman. Obviously I'd felt guilty that my feelings had surfaced while my mother lay in agony, fighting for her life; I imagined that our marriage would be celebrated immediately after Mama died. I had a premonition that my grief would be so painful that only an event like a marriage would have a chance to save me from the depths of oblivion. I would love my young spouse absolutely. I'd find a job. I would establish order in this house. By order, I meant a new order: I would take down walls, change the half-rotted windows, empty the house of its dusty, old-fashioned things, buy new furniture.

Most importantly, I would cut down the oak tree that drowned the house in shadow.

I had started to watch for her arrival with growing malaise, hoped I'd have the courage to approach her and make her understand my intentions. She was aloof with me, and the minute she was inside, she rushed to my mother's room. I of course liked her reserve. She was not a woman easy to approach. That proved to me she was not like other women. And the day when she told me that it was urgent for my mother to be hospitalized I was submerged by the most intense emotion of my life. Even the icy despair that had led me one day to slash my wrists hadn't shaken me so badly. I had to sit down, which impressed the nurse so much that she brought me a glass of water and laid her hand on my shoulder. I drank the water.

Josiane Gravel had explained to me that my mother's days were numbered. She was suffering needlessly. In the hospital she had access to palliative care that would reduce her pain. In fact my mother should have been hospitalized long before but she had rebelled. I understood. She knew the rituals, the torments, the anguish, and the nightmares of death throes prolonged artificially in the name of compassion. Working with the sick for so many years, she was better able to appreciate the distance between a healthy being and another already contaminated by death.

Just as Josiane Gravel laid her hand on my shoulder, I understood that it was now or never. Dry mouthed, I managed to tell her that I would like to marry her as soon as possible, as soon as my mother had succumbed to her illness.

Josiane looked at me, pensive.

I'd thought she was going to accede to my request. My heart leaped in my chest. But she stepped back, suddenly stunned. She moved her head from left to right with small mechanical movements. I stood up to put my arms around her. She slapped me. Apologized at once. I repeated my request, voice quavering. She then looked at me so contemptuously that her spit would have been less hurtful. Her ugliness, which I had grown accustomed to and which over the days had made me feel pity for her but also sympathy that I'd hoped would be transformed into profound affection, that much-loved ugliness now, suddenly, filled me with horror.

Before going back to my mother she had shouted that she already had a fiancé. That was pure spitefulness on her part. Had she guessed that there was no better way to wound me? I was cursing the woman who boasted about coupling with a fiancé and who, with a barely disguised laugh, had rejected me as if I were not worthy of even looking at her. When the ambulance arrived for my mother I saw Josiane again one last time. I noticed then that she dyed her hair. Dark roots betrayed her now questionable blondeness.

While I was travelling in the ambulance with my mother, I was surprised at the fragility of feelings and about their dangerous potential. This woman with whom I had thought I would share my life now turned my stomach. And of that I was ashamed. I was the ugly one, not her.

THE EIFFEL TOWER

Muffled sounds wakened me. Hideous snorting. Like the death rattle of a satanic beast. Though I told myself he was harmless, too weak to hurt me, told myself he really needed help, I hid under the covers like a little boy, hardly daring to breathe.

Who was the man I'd brought to the house, dressed in drag so he'd be taken for a woman? That question rang out in the middle of the night like an alarm. I should have tied him down.

After a long pause, the noise stopped. I switched on my bedside lamp, looking for something to use as a weapon. A miniature replica of the Eiffel Tower stood collecting dust on the chest of drawers opposite my bed. I got up, hefted it. Despite its small size it was heavy enough. A solid blow to the head. Yes. That would do the trick. This stupid object would finally be useful for something.

I tiptoed into my mother's room. Bluish light streaked the man's body. The beach towel lay on the floor. Clutching the Eiffel Tower, I switched on the ceiling light. The man reacted: opened his mouth as if he wanted to tell me something but fainted immediately. I approached him, ready to knock him out. I waited for a long moment. Not the slightest movement, not the slightest groan. How could I be sure he wasn't putting on an act?

I went back to my room, opened the closet, grabbed four neckties, and quickly tied his arms and his legs to the corners of the bed. His body, now in the form of a cross, had lost its muscle tone. Relieved, I touched his forehead. He was burning up. A positive sign: his body was fighting. I covered him with the beach towel and got back into bed.

I didn't fall asleep right away. I had put the miniature Eiffel Tower back on the chest of drawers and now was staring at it. I remembered hating that knick-knack the minute I'd unwrapped it. I'd twisted my face to smile at my mother, who had just given it to me. That she had given it to me proved how well she didn't know me, how dangerous a couple we formed, liable to harm ourselves while thinking we were doing good. She had brought me this souvenir from the only trip she'd ever allowed herself to take. Leaving for a week with a group of nurses, she had visited Paris of course, but also Rome and Venice. She'd come back exhausted but thrilled. I'd never seen her so talkative. Her visit to St. Peter's in Rome had been the high point of her trip. She had breathed the same air as the pope, she exclaimed, still moved, and she'd even touched the tomb of Jean XXIII in the Vatican crypts. But most of all she had been overwhelmed by her visit to a small church where the body of a beatified woman lay in state. She had noticed her glass coffin under the vault of a chapel. The young woman rested in her religious garb. She was as beautiful as a cut flower. My mother didn't understand how a corpse could have stayed so beautiful, so intelligent, so attractive for such a long time. The nun had died more than a century before. With tears in her voice, my mother told me that she had witnessed a genuine miracle. The beatified woman's body had begun to sparkle. The phenomenon had lasted a scant few seconds, a little like a light bulb that, before going out for good, gives off a blast of light.

The story of the beatified woman had first moved me, then frankly it got on my nerves. I had been waiting for my mother for a week, cursing her for leaving me alone. Yet I was no longer a child, I could take care of the house and myself on my own. My mother had explained patiently that this journey had been organized for nurses and that none of them had taken her children. But I couldn't watch Mama leave with her suitcases without wishing her all the woes on earth.

I'd calmed down a few days later by accusing myself of a multitude of lapses, driving a nail into my thigh to punish myself. On her return, when she told me about her emotion at the sight of the glass coffin, something knotted in my stomach. I was angry with my mother for having forgotten me in favour of a dead woman whose body lay incorrupt, a woman eternally dead. After a while, my reaction struck me as infantile but I had nonetheless suffered from it. My distress had till then been so profound that it was a few days after her return that I'd made my pitiful suicide attempt. The miniature Eiffel Tower had long been associated in my mind with that dark period of my life. Kept conspicuously on my chest of drawers, the hated trinket had constituted a sophisticated form of punishment that since then had lost all meaning.

THE FORMULA

I awoke on the stroke of noon. I've always had trouble getting out of bed in the morning. Not from laziness. The beginning of every day gave me a stomach ache. I didn't know about the appetite for life that apparently chimes in the morning amid birdsong and bursts in through curtains flooded with sun. It was not uncommon, especially since my mother's death, for me to rise very late. That morning though someone needed me and I should have gotten up earlier. I rushed into my mother's room.

When I saw him in the light of day, I had a shock. His face, more swollen than the day before, had turned blue. Impressive bruises stained his body with yellow and black.

I did not understand what had happened. I wished my mother were there to enlighten me. I went down to the living room to leaf through her medical encyclopedia that was stored with her cookbooks and novels from a mail-order book club she'd subscribed to. After searching the encyclopedia for fifteen minutes to find an explanation, I had to face facts: I wouldn't find there the case of a young man beaten up by the Four Horsemen of the Apocalypse and skewered with a long branch. I closed the encyclopedia, disappointed. Through the living-room window I could see the letter carrier drop an envelope in the mailbox. I rarely got mail except bills and department-store flyers. Before I went out to pick up the mail, as I was still in my pyjamas, I checked to see if neighbours could see me. Rather rare at this time of year, a woman was raking the first fallen leaves from her lawn. When she bent over to stuff the leaves into an orange plastic bag, I used the moment to get my mail. Then, suddenly, she raised her head. I felt miserable. No doubt about it, she'd seen me. I realized that being in pyjamas after noon was suspicious behaviour that encouraged a negative interpretation.

The letter was from the cemetery where my mother had been interred. The management thanked me for calling on their services, asked if I was satisfied, reminded me that nine months had passed since the sad event, hoped that time had healed my sorrow, and finally, suggested a personalized plan that included anniversary Masses, flowers, maintenance of the grave, with significant reductions if, of course, I took advantage of this exceptional offer before December 1.

What bothered me most about the promotional offer was the anniversary Masses. I had no appetite for insipid, excruciating rituals and I saw nothing that my presence would contribute to a Mass. Basically, the Church had nothing to do with my mother's soul or with how God would look at that soul and its eternal rest. I conducted my business with God in a personal manner. My Our Fathers were in my opinion a thousand times more genuine than the sermons of a priest.

I tore up the letter, feeling that my mother's remains belonged to me less and less, that they were in the hands of an institution that was managing her like some inter-changeable thing. Place flowers on her grave, pull weeds, clear snow in winter – it was little compared with every-thing my mother had done for me. I had no need of any promotional offer to honour her memory. I would care for her grave by myself. And I'd look after the young man by myself. I would find the way to heal him, I didn't need anyone. Besides, his condition was improving. The bluish tinge to his face showed that something was going on under his skin. It was as simple as that: something was working non-stop to rebuild muscles, repair damaged tissues. The pus and the discharges due to lacerations and hematomas were gradually being expelled. Bad blood would soon be eliminated through the pores. I just had to study my poor stigmata to understand to what degree the skin can care for itself. The young man was working on his own recovery. Calmed by that thought, I went back to my mother's room.

THE CONDOM

I opened the window for air and studied his puffy face. My hopes crumbled: this young man was not on the road to healing. The bluish tint of his face had nothing to do with the bruises on his body, nothing to do with the normal expulsion of subcutaneous waste. This young man, I was certain, was suffocating.

I bent over him to better hear his breathing, reduced now to a disturbing high-pitched wheeze. Could it be that by tying down his feet and hands I had blocked the young man's circulation? After a quick look, I realized I hadn't knotted the neckties too tightly. Something was wrong. I opened his mouth and noticed an impressive amount of saliva at the back of his throat. Was he drowning? I went to the kitchen for my rubber gloves, but once there, I remembered I'd thrown them out the day before. I raced back up to him, howling an Our Father, stuck my forefinger in his mouth. I dug around as best I could at the back of his throat to clear out the saliva, which was thick as glue. I was wiping my finger on the beach towel when he suffered a spasm followed by a groan. He opened his mouth, frantically. It was obvious he was trying to breathe. Again I inserted my finger in his mouth, at the back of his throat where I touched something remarkably soft. I made pincers with my thumb and forefinger and pulled the thing. For a moment I thought I'd just extricated a piece of his own flesh. Then I realized, stupefied, that what I had in my hand was a condom. I raced to the bathroom to vomit. With my head in the bowl, I no longer doubted that the young man, despite his sexual deviance, warranted all the compassion I'd never been able to give anyone. I mustn't think about the fact that he had on woman's clothes, the obvious reason for his current ordeal. The outrages he had suffered were beyond understanding. His suffering appeared to me as a vast wounded field where, as far as the eye could see, evil contaminated the skies.

THE EYE

Two days later he was doing better. I had thrown out
the beach towel, got rid of the floral print bedspread,
put the young man to bed between clean sheets, bought
an antiseptic ointment to disinfect his sores. I gave
him some apple juice to drink. After long hesitation
I decided to feed him some vegetables. I fixed puréed
potatoes and carrots but he spat them out. I tried my
luck with strawberries in yogurt. He swallowed a few
good spoonsful. His face had lost its bluish tint and the
swelling was going down. I freed him from the neckties that kept him motionless. I had no need to protect
myself from an inert doll. Yet his face was almost ani-
mated. Sometimes he opened his eyes, but his gaze was
still vague. He slept most of the time, moaned, wakened,
went back to sleep. Eventually I managed to feed him
some cereal in hot milk.

The shock to his head that he'd suffered must certainly
have after-effects. He waved his arms but I'd never seen
him move his legs. His position in the bed varied only
slightly. Mornings, I found him as I'd seen him the night
before. At times I thought I saw a vague smile. I chased
away that idea. In his present state and after such humili-
ation, how could he smile?

At nightfall I opened my bedroom window to let
in some fresh autumn air with its odour of damp earth.
I bundled up in my blankets and asked God's forgiveness

for my lapses, my weaknesses, my pettiness. I had made the decision to devote myself body and soul to the young man. He had nothing to do with me, I had no reason to behave as I was doing. This astounding absence of logic filled me with a sense of euphoria. I was walking in the footsteps of those who are liberated from their self-esteem, their narcissism, their selfishness.

Once, I lifted the lid of one of his eyes. Captivated by its vacant stare, green verging on yellow, I felt as if I were discovering a precious stone. The eye was living by itself, apart from any human expression; then a shiver ran down my spine from head to toe: it had just looked at me. His eye had come to life with a presence so dense that I left the room. In a flash I had caught a glimpse of the man's soul. My consciousness had plunged, beyond the liquid green of his eye, into everything he'd experienced since birth. As if I'd been in contact with thousands of thoughts and memories that had never belonged to me, thousands of sensations and emotions I had never felt. I had just recognized in that singular gaze all the hatred I thought I myself had tasted. A moment of disgusting attraction as quick as a stabbing. This man was not just anybody. He had committed acts whose searing intensity I suspected but without speaking a word about them.

I dared not open his eyes again.

THE BIBLE

Before she put me to bed my mother used to read me passages from the Bible. She knew she couldn't count on public school for my religious education. One night she told me the story of the massacre of the Holy Innocents: the Three Magi having warned Herod of the coming of a new king, he ordered that all male children in the region of Bethlehem under two years of age be killed.

As a little boy, my sleep had been disturbed. Images of children killed by soldiers hounded me. Under my closed eyelids, harrowing visions fought for space: corpses of babies, bloody and pierced by two-edged swords and lances, arms and heads cut off; the mothers' laments; the snickering of soldiers. Why had the birth of Christ required the death of thousands of children? I had asked my mother. She'd answered that the life of Christ was worth a thousand times more than the life of any child. I didn't understand. Sometime later I announced to my mother that I wanted to be a priest. I didn't have enough imagination at the time to prove my love to her any other way. Most of all, I was jealous of Christ, of his suffering that was worth a thousand times more than mine. I wanted to suffer more than He had ever suffered. For a long time my nights had been filled with nightmares when I revisited the sacrifice of children torn from their mothers.

That forgotten period of my childhood had resurfaced unexpectedly on the death of my paternal grandfather. At his funeral, my grandmother gave me a book he'd written in his youth. "Here," she'd told me, "you'll soon be as old as he was when he wrote it. I'm sure he'd have wanted you to read it." I kissed my grandmother, whom I never saw again, and left with my inheritance from my grandfather under my arm.

It was a travel diary published at his own expense. My grandfather had kept it during his visit to India in 1940. One passage in particular struck my imagination. My grandfather was in Goa, a Portuguese colony at the time. He had gone into a church in a coastal village, wishing to attend a Mass to communicate with the soul of his mother, who had died several months before his departure. During the service, his gaze had been attracted by the impressive crucifix hanging over the altar. Christ's pain struck him as hideous. "How could I have worshipped a man being tortured, torn apart on a cross, face ravaged, gaze imploring?" The day before, he had visited a Hindu temple. He had left highly impressed, fascinated by the festive excitement of this sacred place where hundreds of people strolled amid statues glistening with ghee, covered with flower petals. He was profoundly convinced: one could not live at peace with oneself by kneeling before the image of weakness and renunciation represented by Christ crucified. His suffering wouldn't save the world. Suffering was the most useless thing in Creation. It was better, wrote my grandfather, who was then a young man, to stun oneself amid the unusual vitality of Hindu deities. Why couldn't gods dance, sing, laugh?

Reading that passage had reminded me of the fright provoked in me as a child by the story of the massacre of the Holy Innocents. My grandfather was vindicated: Christ's suffering was no more important than mine. No one should suffer and die for Him, especially not children.

I had no need of Christ, I had my Our Fathers.

THE FILM

I now called him *Jean* in honour of Jean XXIII, my mother's favourite pope. Every day for a month I had been checking the progress of his recovery. His superficial wounds were practically healed. The bruises had paled. I memorized every scratch, every abrasion. I even picked at his thickest scabs. For that kind of operation I wore rubber gloves of which I'd bought a good supply. The same for his daily ablutions. As I got used to tolerating this new intimacy, I eventually dropped the rubber gloves, simply disinfecting my hands. After a while I didn't even bother to do that.

I knew that being confined to bed could cause bed-sores. It wasn't my mother who taught me that; I'd seen it in a film on TV: a story about a deranged woman who, to punish her husband who'd left her for another, made her child sick by poisoning her a little at a time. The child spent months in bed before she died. What struck me most in the story was precisely the term *bedsores* the coroner used at the trial. The woman was accused not only of poisoning her own daughter but also of not changing her position in bed, which in the eyes of the prosecutor proved beyond the shadow of a doubt the perversity of the accused. Though more than twenty years had passed since I'd seen the film, I only had to close my eyes and I would see again the photos of the child that the prosecutor showed the jury, photos in which bedsores were clearly visible, circled in red. Had I over the years transformed the scenario so grotesquely? Could be. But the main thing was the special attention I paid to the expression *bedsores,* as if the bed itself were suffering, with wounds oozing blood and pus. And that was why, when my mother took sick, I had told Josiane Gravel way more than necessary to change her position in the bed so that she wouldn't be afflicted with them. I had repeated that so often in such a short time that the nurse, inevitably exasperated but not showing it to me, would have been absolutely right to think I was losing my mind, considering that bedsores don't form overnight as I learned later. Suspecting that I could disturb Jean by constantly turning him over in his bed as I did on the first days – which moreover demanded a tremendous physical effort – I had finally looked in the medical encyclopedia for the hidden meaning behind the expression *bedsores.* The description was reassuring. The sore didn't appear all that easily, it took time. As a precaution however I decided to systematically change Jean's position every Tuesday and Saturday.

Washing his soiled sheets and diapers was an ordeal for me. I would pinch my nose, hold back my tears, and for hours afterwards I'd be unable to ingest the smallest bit of food. After a while I started to take pride in it and to feel an impressive tranquility. The daily jobs brought me closer to my mother. Had she not, for years, performed the same tasks as a nurse? And at the end of her life had she not had to agree to exchange roles, to be washed, changed, cared for by the hands of strangers? I discovered that performing those same tasks for a person, even if it was for just a few days, I would be better able to understand him than if we'd spent a lifetime together.

THE WAREHOUSE

Taking advantage of a moment's lucidity, I had asked my dying mother why, on my seventh birthday, she'd thrown out everything that had belonged to my father and never again mentioned his name or his existence. I hoped naively that her answer would bring me back my life, as if she had cheated at my birth, leaving her womb only an empty shell that she'd called Edgar, a name as hard as a piece of charred wood. But she never answered. Even during the last moments of her life, eyes darkened with pain, intubated, bluish marks on her arms in places where her veins had ruptured under skin that was too thin, she hadn't wanted to tell her son the truth, hadn't wanted to confide in him what painful secret her dried-up heart was keeping. She had preferred that silence engulf us both with her last breath.

After she died I searched the house for a clue that would help me understand what had led her to erase the memory of my father after she had maintained it so zealously for so many years. For throughout my childhood she had played her role of widow by elaborating for her son a golden image of her husband. I found nothing in the drawers or in the cartons rotting in the cellar. I felt ashamed as I inspected her clothes, even breaking the little padlock on a sandalwood box where she had kept her worthless jewellery and cards sent by patients to show their gratitude. Perhaps a part of my mother continued to exist in the bedroom, scene of her suffering. Maybe she'd seen me rummaging through her possessions.

What do we know of the dead?

She had died in January. She couldn't have chosen a worse time. Thirty below zero, city buried in snow, gusts of wind. They'd had to store her remains in a warehouse. I'd had to wait for the spring thaw to watch her coffin descend into the earth. There was no one but me at this belated ceremony, aside from two dozing employees of the cemetery and a priest mumbling words of comfort.

When I came home from the funeral, I went up to her room, kissed her bed where the impression of her body could still be seen. I bade her farewell. If my mother still had the slightest particle of existence it was with God, not in this bedroom. But for all that, I was not free of my suspicions about the stubbornness of souls. Some weeks later I removed a photo of my mother wearing her nurse's uniform from my bookcase, where it took pride of place. I'd had it framed as a gift for her fortieth birthday. Not daring to throw it out, I had stuffed it in the cellar in a carton full of old clothes. I had also planned to empty her drawers and her cupboards and throw everything out. Finally, everything stayed where it was. My mother could have come back from the dead and found her things where she had stored them.

THE BEARD

Jean was still eating very little but he was accepting food more willingly. To feed him I sat him up with a pillow wedged behind his back. After a while his head would drop to his chest, a sign he was exhausted. I would lay him down horizontally and finish feeding him as best I could.

His beard was a constant concern. It soaked up food and liquid, forcing me to clean it several times a day. I could have solved the problem by cutting it but I couldn't persuade myself to do that. Jean had become Jean when his beard appeared. I combed it and enjoyed doing that. It was my work. Besides, Jean's blondness lit up his face, concealing any sign of the blows he'd received from his assailants. I was surprised to be giving it so much importance. Never had a man attracted my gaze because he had a beard. I had known some bearded men of course, professors or the psychologist my mother had forced me to consult. Most sported a moustache. My paternal grandfather had worn a beard at the end of his life.

As for me, it was not until I turned twenty that I saw a few timid hairs on my chin and I had to shave weekly. It was actually better that I didn't have to suffer the shaving ritual every morning because as soon as I had a razor in my hand, I felt the need to cut my skin. Aside from the two or three times I'd chosen a nail, I had always used a razor blade to mutilate myself. I cut my thighs and upper arms. I had never done it on my face even though at one time

I was obsessed with the desire to slash my lips. I imagined the scene where I showed up in the living room when my mother, home from work, was watching her weekly quiz show. I didn't make her howl right away. I gave her time to get up, look at me with total incomprehension. Then I spoke the word *mama*, a word drowned immediately in blood, a word buried at once in my mother's cry. My fantasy never went beyond that cry. I had described it one day to the psychologist who was treating me. I thought I was pathetic. That production, unfurling in front of him in the form of sentences and not squeezed into the privacy of my conscience, had struck me as so ridiculous that subsequently, never again was I tempted to go there.

By being confronted every day with the disturbing reality of the human body, with its smells and its eruptions, its metamorphoses and secrets, I rediscovered at times the tumult of my teen years. But a depth was added to it that moved me, gave me the feeling that I had not survived in vain my obsessions, my dark ideas. Now it was Jean who was suffering. He was doing it for my soul. While I washed away his excrement, disinfected his sores, cleaned his sheets, he took charge of my decline, absorbed it, purified it. I reached the point where I couldn't get along without the moments I devoted to him, so much so that I had to discipline myself. Observing a plant for twelve hours in a row will not make it grow faster, so I checked my outbursts, and deliberately spent time on the main floor when I would have preferred to stay in Jean's room from morning till night.

THE NOTEBOOK

A few months after my mother's funeral I had received a large envelope in the mail. I was about to open it when I felt a twinge of sorrow: the return address bore the name Josiane Gravel.

I set the envelope on the kitchen table.

A whirlwind of thoughts paralyzed me. In the best-case scenario I imagined Josiane Gravel repenting her attitude, leaving me with the hope of seeing her again. In the worst, I assumed she hadn't been able to stop herself from writing me a heap of insults, accompanied by threats from her fiancé, whom she must have married by now. Then I became aware of the stupidity of my suppositions, of their disproportion, their unlikelihood, especially because I'd never thought about the woman again. I was dismayed by my fragility, by the emotion that was devastating me at the sight of the envelope. I circled the table for a long moment before opening it.

Josiane Gravel wrote that my mother, weakened by disease and unable to do it herself, had begged her to destroy a notebook. She couldn't remember where she had stored it. Josiane Gravel had found it in a hat box. The next day my mother had left the house by ambulance. Josiane Gravel hadn't completed her task, the notebook was inside the envelope.

I went and sat in the living-room easy chair. I could hear my heart beating loudly. If my mother, so deeply confused that she didn't know who I was, or so it seemed, in a last burst of consciousness had gathered up her past and the little bit of life still in her to recall the existence of the notebook – then immediately remove it from my comprehension – it meant that in one way or another it must concern me, might harm me.

After a long moment I went back to the kitchen, took the notebook out of the envelope, breathed in its aroma. I had thought I would detect my mother's scent. I smelled nothing but a whiff of dust, a vaguely stuffy odour. I opened its cover and recognized her writing: strictly ordered sentences, words close together as if they stood at the edge of a precipice. Notes she had taken during her nursing studies about syringes, the bloodstream ... I skimmed them all before coming to some pages written a few years later. It wasn't the future nurse who had put them on paper but a young girl named Anne-Marie Létourneau who was preparing to marry a man named Alexis Trudel and who gave birth a year later to a son named Edgar Trudel, a son who had the impression, reading the young woman's notebook, that he had never known his mother.

Anne-Marie.

I'd never called her that. If I had even once, both our lives would have been sweeter.

On the last pages of the notebook my mother described her wedding night and the apprehensions that had come before. She took an obvious pleasure in describing her feelings, multiplying breathless phrases about the physical features of her future husband. It upset me. A passage in which she talked about her own sex as a fragile, breakable object was a disgrace. Ridiculous.

My mother quite immodestly opened up about her heart and her body, describing the hunger that gnawed at her, hunger for her Alexis. She could not sleep, she was a virgin, her future husband had surely known other women, she was afraid of appearing awkward. To prepare herself she had read books, watched films, discussed those matters with her colleagues at the hospital where she'd just been hired. I discovered that my mother had been in her own way obsessed with sex, yet she talked about it as if she were living in the nineteenth century. There was no end to her admiration of the power that emanated from the arms of her Alexis. She had danced with him, snuggled up against his thighs, liked the tobacco smell on his clothes, went so far as to declare that she could get used to his breath. These details made me unhappy, but the passages recounting her wedding night shattered me. Her Alexis had been unbelievably brutal with her. In order to come, he had called her a whore, hit her. My mother had cried all night, silently, for fear of waking him. Her sex was bleeding, she was afraid of dying but dared not get out of bed. At dawn her brand new husband had behaved as if they were the happiest couple in the world. My mother pointed out that she had rinsed her husband's pyjamas and her own nightgown in the bathroom sink. She even soaked the sheets in the bathtub, ashamed that employees of the hotel where they were staying might regard indignantly the remains of their wedding night.

I was shaken. I had the feeling that the house had just split in two, releasing a cry of rage from the cellar. I went to my mother's room, opened the closet, and touched the hat box where, according to Josiane Gravel, my mother had hidden her notebook.

After her death I had searched that closet and I had a very clear memory of that box, which I had emptied: three outmoded hats, a pair of white kid gloves, and a yellowed photograph. I had put everything back in place. I hadn't paid much attention to the photo. I had recognized my mother. She must have been very young and she was standing next to a man I had taken to be her father. They'd been photographed in front of a house that I did not recognize. Now that I had the photo before my eyes again I could see better. What an idiot I was! The man standing next to my mother wasn't her father but mine. The broad-shouldered man with the wide forehead was her future husband. The date on the back of the photo noted that it had been taken two months before their marriage. Now I made the connection between that austere face with the harsh expression and the one that I saw in the mirror: I looked like my father. My mother had made no mistake on that score, she who'd repeated so often that as I got older I could be his "spitting image." That was of course before she got rid of all his things and erased his memory from our lives.

If I had never known my father, who died on the day I was born, I doubted now that I had known my mother, who had died on her wedding night.

THE CEMETERY

In the photo my mother looked frail, smiling faintly as
if expressing some secret victory. My father at her side
gave the impression of an immovable block. There was
a little snow on the ground, left by the spring thaw. It
must have been cold that day, yet my mother had on
only a light sweater over her dress, while my father wore
his winter coat. He was frowning, blinded by the sun.
Mainly, he looked profoundly bored. Why had she kept
that one photo and thrown out all the others? I had no
answer but I understood that a bridal photo, after what
I'd learned about her wedding night, would have been
too painful to look at.

That day I put the notebook and the photo back in the
hat box and went directly to the cemetery. At that time
I hadn't been there since my mother's funeral in the spring.

Evening was approaching, scented by the flowers
fading on all the tombs. The August light was wavering in
the sky. I was astonished to feel relieved. While looking
for my mother's grave I caught myself thinking about
Josiane Gravel again. What had got into me, asking her
to marry me? I'd said barely two words to her during the
weeks when she had taken care of my mother. At the
heart of the cemetery the sounds of the city gave way
to the song of crickets, the air was blue, the shadows
on the ground very soft. Kneeling close to the black
marble plaque where gold letters spelled out her married

name – ANNE-MARIE TRUDEL – I made my mother a declaration of love. I knew her painful secret. Her husband hadn't respected her. He had called her a whore on her wedding night. She had spent her life trying to erase the memory of it. That evening I took the measure of all the pain I'd made her suffer and all the good she'd given me in return. I knew it now: I had not been a child of love. How many humiliating nights had her Alexis subjected her to? God bless Josiane for sending me that notebook! I could see clearly: I was born of a transgression my mother had suffered, a wound she'd kept warm in her belly.

I got in the habit of coming to her grave every day. Reading the notebook had convinced me of one thing: my birth had freed her of her torturer. I had been her saviour.

I started several letters to Josiane Gravel that I tore up before they were finished. I wanted to thank her for her daring in sending me the notebook. I could have accused her of reading it, of intruding. How could I thank her and at the same time not accuse her? Above all, I was dying to know why she'd thought it right that I should read the notebook. The woman definitely intrigued me and the feelings I'd had for her earlier now regained a hint of their slight, passing vigour, an exquisite torment. Was it possible that Josiane Gravel had felt a little affection, a ghost of regret for having slapped me, that she had felt pity for the son when reading what his mother had endured?

I finally entered a stationery shop to find a birthday card. I chose the most ordinary: it showed a cake with candles. Inside I wrote these few words: *I know it's not your birthday but when that day arrives you will have in reserve this card and my wishes that go with it. Thank you for the notebook. It has changed my life.* I hesitated to send it, appalled that an act as simple as mailing a letter could upset me so much. I waited till evening to go out. I took the car and drove across town before I found the courage to put it in a mailbox. Josiane Gravel had to know that as I'd written to her on the card, my life was no longer the same. I was not the human wreck she'd slapped and sneered at. My birth had provoked the death of the man who had humiliated, who had soiled my mother.

The letter finally mailed, I went to the cemetery. I knelt on my mother's grave and talked to her about Josiane Gravel, about the new impulses the name now stirred in me. The more I talked the more my emotion grew, giving weight to my hope for a better life, a life my mother would have been proud of, an orderly life without suffering, without shame, lived in the light and under the eyes of others.

That night I fell asleep on her grave. I never suspected that hope would fly away and disappear forever in the hours to come. I was wakened by the sadistic laughter of four men, Four Horsemen of the Apocalypse whose appalling crime would change the course of my life, relegating the memory of Josiane Gravel to the shadow of the man I would call Jean. My visits to the graveyard had immediately lost all interest, as had the desire to please a woman.

THE CANDLE

On Halloween, I had switched off all the lights in the house. I wasn't anxious to have monsters ring my doorbell. I didn't want any indiscreet glances. I was on my guard, looking out the window at passersby I considered suspicious because they turned their heads in the direction of the house. I was afraid that I'd be arrested, that they'd take Jean away. After all, the man must have relatives, friends, a job. His disappearance must have been reported. Someone in this town must be looking for him. He could be married and – why not? – have children. Even though he had been dressed like a woman, I did not let myself judge him. Spoon-feeding him like a child had relieved him in my eyes of any form of vice. Ever since his beard had grown, the fact that I had confused him with a woman struck me as inconceivable.

No light came in through the curtains. I listened to Jean's breathing in the dark. It seemed to be coming from me. I guessed at the phenomenal amount of energy needed to remain oneself, guessed that it took only a moment's inattention, a passing weakness to slip between the cracks as if one were someone else.

I had the feeling I was merging with him, plunging to the heart of his suffering, tasting it, eating it like a meal. The bedroom sunk in darkness closed me within its mystery, digested me in its womb. As I listened to Jean's breathing, I heard my own life. I was born again as if the room were giving birth to another Edgar, born of no parent, born rather of this man who was breathing the darkness of my past. I wanted to think what he thought, to wander in his closed head. I wanted a sign from him.

I lit a candle. The glimmer of the little flame made my shadow dance on the walls. My gaze was drawn to the mark left by the crucifix above the bed. The room was beginning to look like a sanctuary where Jean ruled like a sleeping enigma. I was struck by the fair colour of his beard, which in the half-light gave his face a new intensity. I found myself suddenly in the presence of a man who had suffered, a man whose face had stolen the features of Christ. I leaned across, placed my lips on his brow for a long time. A sense of plenitude swept over me. At last, I was tasting peace. Straightening up, I saw my mother. She had taken Jean's place. She was howling but no sound came from her mouth. I left the room, rushed to the stairs, missed a step, fell, pulled myself up, and at top speed ran out into the night.

THE STAIN

I had taken refuge in a bus shelter. Left without a coat, shivering. I considered myself a coward for running away like a child. Why should I have been afraid of my mother? She was dead and buried. No hallucination would bring her back from the land of the deceased. I tried to compose myself but that vision had shaken me. I felt guilty: and if I were the assailant, the one who'd beaten Jean in the cemetery, who'd kicked, humiliated, soiled him … If it were me? … I was losing my mind. I had to get a grip. I was accusing myself of something impossible.

A group of children strolled down the sidewalk. A young girl extracted herself from the group and headed for the bus shelter. Her gait was strangely light, as if she were skipping. She asked if I needed help. Maybe she thought I was homeless. That must have been what I looked like. She was holding a little Halloween pumpkin, though she wasn't in costume. Instead of answering her question, I stared at her. Her beauty frightened me. She thrust her hand into her pumpkin, offered me a candy, then went off to join her group. That was when I noticed that she was wearing, fastened to her back, two tiny wings. I unwrapped the angel's candy and stuffed it in my mouth. I felt better.

When I finally got back to the house my clothes were soaked with cold sweat. My teeth were chattering. I took a cautious look around Jean's room. Everything seemed normal, no more apparitions. I ran a very hot bath. The warmth enveloped me. Closing my eyes, I let the tears flow. I saw again the children in costumes of the living dead or ghosts, especially the little girl with tiny wings. My thoughts raced ahead: the massacre of the Holy Innocents, my grandfather, his rebellion before the image of the crucifixion, the mystery of suffering … Perhaps he and I were wrong. And did the coming of Christ merit the deaths of thousands of children?

Children like those I had just seen.

When I opened my eyes again there was a lot of blood in the tub. Hurrying out of the water I dried myself while trying to see where the blood was coming from. I had one scraped elbow and two or three bruises on my legs, a result of my recent fall on the stairs, but no bleeding wounds. I pulled the plug. Maybe I would discover something abnormal as the water flowed … It was only when I saw the final swirl rush down the drain that I was aware of my stupidity. What did I hope to find? One of my organs that, I don't know how, had managed to break away from my body?

I lay down. Immediately, a multitude of thoughts swept over me. I chased them away, they came back via circuitous routes as if everything I had done was just a subterfuge to take me back to square one: I had just lost some blood without knowing the cause or feeling any effect. And this time I was sure it wasn't a hallucination.

Something had bled in my bath, something that came from elsewhere: that was what I kept concluding.

I switched on my bedside lamp. Sitting up in my bed I watched for the slightest indication of the presence in my room of a being that hadn't been invited, a being no longer human that had once been part of the world but now lived in squalor. I recalled the terror that vampire films plunged me into when I was a child. Those lugubrious stories had introduced me to the existence of evil: beings inhabited by death that grabbed hold of the living and forced them to behave abjectly. Evil had more weight than good. And as vampires sucked their victims' blood when they were sleeping, I imagined that evil entered me during my sleep, wending its way inside my veins to my heart, where it took root. Sleeping was the most dangerous thing I could do. Yet in the morning I noted that once again I had succumbed to sleep regardless of my childlike vigilance.

Still thinking about that time, I had to sleep in spite of everything. I woke up sitting in my bed, the bedside light on. As soon as I was up I went to Jean's room and opened the drawer where I'd put my mother's crucifix. After what had happened the night before, I insisted on putting it back in its place. A surprise awaited me. I found it at the back of a drawer, in two pieces. The Christ and his cross had been severed into almost equal sizes, as if someone had used a saw at the level of his navel. For a moment I imagined that Jean had … No, once again fear was leading me to some outlandish suppositions. I took the pieces down to the kitchen and glued them together. That little job completed, I realized that I'd never really looked at the crucifix. It had always looked down in sorrow on my mother's bed. Christ's face, twisted in pain, lips partly open, was begging for help.

I went to the living room, jammed the crucifix between the two biggest books I could find on the library shelves. In an hour or two it would be fixed. I went up to my room to change. As soon as I entered I saw a stain on my sheets in the place where I'd fallen asleep, sitting up. I took off my pyjama bottoms and turned them inside out: there too was a stain. No doubt about it, it was blood. I dashed to the bathroom and examined myself in the mirror. Nothing out of the ordinary, but that only increased my anxiety.

Around noon I went to pick up the crucifix. A little dried glue had dropped onto the wood. I took a knife and scraped it. Went upstairs. Climbed onto the bed, stepping over Jean. Just as I was hanging the crucifix on its nail, Jean grabbed me by the leg. Unbalanced, I landed on the floor on all fours. I looked up in Jean's direction; he seemed calm. Definitely, his condition was improving. I wasn't sure if I was thrilled at the thought. I liked Jean immobile, silent. I had noticed with apprehension that he could now move his legs. I suspected him of getting up at night. I no longer had a choice: I bought a chain to attach him securely to his bed.

CHICKEN POT PIE

My mother had always fixed my meals. In spite of her job at the hospital, even during her long illness before she was bedridden. Weekends, she was in the habit of making quiches, lasagnes, pies, and soups that she froze in numbered plastic containers. Each figure corresponded to a type of food: 1 for quiche, 2 for soups, 3 for lasagna … When she came home from work she never failed to ask what I'd eaten at noon. My reply would be a number: I'd had some 3, or 4, or 5. It made her smile. It was one of the few rituals that brought us together.

That day marked a year since my mother's death and nearly four months I'd been living with Jean. Winter was as icy as the year before. I would walk around the house wrapped in a blanket. I opened the freezer compartment in the fridge. It had occurred to me that there might still be one of my mother's precooked dishes. I found one hidden behind some ice-cube trays. I held it upside down deliberately so I wouldn't see the number on the lid. I smiled sadly when I realized that one year after her death I was going to eat the last meal my mother had cooked for me. I had the painful sensation I was holding my mother's frozen remains, as if a little of her flesh, of her nasty kindness, her dry, precise hands, a little of the person she had been could be found in that plastic container. I imagined that a short distance from where I was now, under the cold, damp January earth, my mother's body had the same toughness, the same appearance – like tightly compressed and frozen food – as the plate I held in my hands. I no longer felt sad, and it appalled me.

I finally turned the container upside down, looked at the number on the lid: 4. Chicken pot pie.

I put it in the microwave. Twenty minutes later I sampled the pie, its insipid taste that resembled nothing. I forced myself to eat it despite my urge to vomit. I kept a small portion for Jean, went upstairs. I hoped, naively, that this uncommon communion might bring us together: my mother, him, and me. But Jean spat it out, unaccustomed to this kind of food. I had left it in the microwave too long and the crust was tough. I took a mouthful, chewed it for a long time, pressed my lips to Jean's, and passed the food from my mouth to his.

I went down to the kitchen to wash the empty plastic container. I couldn't stand still. I was taken over by a sudden urge to paint the entire house, to lose myself in household tasks I had put off doing. I was jubilant, exultant. Never would I have thought joy could achieve that dimension.

THE SECOND NOTEBOOK

Usually I washed Jean in bed. I used two basins, one filled with soapy water, the other with hot water in which I rinsed my washcloth. That system spared me going back and forth constantly between bathroom and bedroom. On Sundays I gave him a shampoo. Then I would spend part of the day washing the dirty clothes amassed during the week. Anyway, I've never liked Sunday, so I might as well spend it performing unpleasant tasks.

I'm not sure why on that particular morning I felt like giving Jean a real bath. I helped him walk to the bathroom and get into the tub. His scrawniness touched me. I couldn't help seeing in his body the suffering body of Christ. It was absurd, I knew that, and though I reasoned with myself, I was stirred as if the body I was washing were also his, were also the body of the Jesus I'd been jealous of, whose suffering I had felt suspect. I'd been wrong to ridicule his silent suffering because I thought I'd seen it in any man, any woman, any insect crushed underfoot. But I had confused it with pain, so easily made to appear in the body, whereas suffering was the very flesh of the human soul. Without it there would be no soul; without it, life would have no value and anyone at all, acting impulsively, could be rid of it, considering it pointless.

I stripped and got into the tub. Jean was immediately intrigued by the scars that streaked my arms and legs. Silently, without speaking, he examined them at length, then ran his finger over them as if he were looking for a message buried in my flesh. Uneasy, I soaped him from head to toe, rinsed him off, put him back to bed, and chained him up.

I went to the kitchen to fix him something to eat. I saw then through the window that the letter carrier had left an envelope in my mailbox.

In a letter more detailed than the first, Josiane Gravel told me something astonishing: there actually existed two notebooks. Another surprising thing was that my mother, whom she'd visited in the hospital several times, kept changing her mind about the notebooks. One day she insisted that Josiane Gravel destroy them, the next day that she give them to me after her death. As the days went by she had become more and more confused, until she'd forgotten all about the notebooks. In the end, Josiane Gravel hadn't destroyed them. After my mother died, she had read them. Wanting to respect my mother's last wishes but not knowing what they were, she felt authorized. She had waited several months before sending me the first notebook, thinking the pain of my grief at my mother's death by that time would be less intense.

Josiane Gravel wrote that she had not mentioned to me the existence of the second notebook and never would have if my greeting card hadn't reassured her. I had written that reading the notebook had "changed my life," and those words had convinced her that she should send me the second one too. "Today is my birthday, I've given myself the gift of seeing this matter through to the end," she wrote at the end of her letter.

The second notebook was smaller than the first. The first page was covered with the letter *a* written awkwardly in pencil. A lined exercise book, that of a six-year-old taking his first steps as he learns to write. I felt a pang; I had been that child. I turned the pages, saw a series of *b*s, of *c*s, of *d*s. After that came something else: the dense handwriting of my mother appeared, in her violet ink. I went to the living room and read the last ten pages without stopping.

My mother accused herself of wanting to kill me.

It was clean, clear, written with no hesitation. She had tried to drown her two-year-old child in his bath.

She had held my head under water. I couldn't believe it. I searched my recollections for a shred of memory that could have been related to that scene, I found nothing, recalled nothing. My mother though had repeated her foul attempt, holding my head under water longer each time, as if she were in training. She had loved her husband so much, she wrote, there was nothing left for a son. My birth had expelled her Alexis from the world, as if from the outset there had never been enough room on earth for him and me. One or the other but not both. I was born, he died, through my fault. She had learned to love him, she hadn't had to learn to hate me. With God's help she had reined in her violence against me but the memory of her husband haunted her, rekindling her bitterness. I got bigger, walked, talked, became everything for her but, most of all, I was her permanent punishment. She'd given birth to a son she wanted to kill, she had to atone for that.

When I reached the age of six, she felt the beginning of relief. Her work at the hospital, where she'd gone back full time, and my starting primary school gave her life a new impetus. A year later, she threw out everything that reminded her of her husband, tore up his photos, never uttered his name in my presence again, never recalled his memory. She had accepted her role as a mother.

"I learned to love Alexis the way a little dog learns to love her master. I still love him. I don't forgive myself."

Those two statements, which end the notebook, caused me more pain than all the others together. My birth had been a bereavement. How my mother must have detested me when she gave me her breast! How she must have detested my birthdays that reminded her more of the day she'd become a widow than of the one when she'd become a mother!

BAGS

I made a pile in the middle of the living room with all the objects, knick-knacks, pictures, souvenirs that had belonged to her. I emptied the kitchen drawers of all the cumbersome, useless little things my mother had accumulated: key rings, embroidered doilies, decks of cards, spools of thread. I pulled down her collection of fridge magnets. I took out of their dusty vases the even dustier dried flowers she'd arranged on the kitchen table and the small table in the living room. I took several garbage bags up to the bathroom. Emptied the medicine chest of its poor-quality cosmetics, cheap perfumes, bottles of expired pills, tubes of dried ointment, a bottle of sickeningly pink nail polish, two old toothbrushes. In her room I cleared the wardrobe and drawers of her dresses, coats, smelly underwear, ridiculous hats, worn-out shoes reeking of sadness. I came down to the living room with three garbage bags stuffed with clothing and trinkets. I filled other bags with most of the books in the bookcase: yellowed volumes; never-opened novels from her famous mail-order collection of the classics; dog-eared women's magazines; stained, greasy cookbooks. In less than an hour I had piled ten full garbage bags in the middle of the living room. The garbage men wouldn't come for another two days. I opened the cellar door and dropped the bags down the stairs one at a time. I had decided to leave only two on the curb at a time, each week the garbage men came. A huge pile of garbage would have attracted attention.

I wasn't keen to have the neighbours notice anything about my house. At this rate I would be rid of the garbage bags in a matter of weeks. I went out to get groceries. Surprised myself buying new and more expensive things. Went back to the house with a flank steak instead of the ground beef that before I would have consumed as meatballs. I also bought fruit for Jean. Winter slowed the city behind frosted windows. I whistled silly tunes. I felt light.

A week later, everything changed dramatically.

Jean was burning up with fever. His room was filled with a sour smell. He refused all food. I'd freed him of his chain and buried him under a mound of blankets. He moaned, his teeth chattered. It was unbearable. I dissolved some aspirins in a glass of water and managed to make him take a few sips. Washing him, I discovered his lymph nodes had grown to an enormous size. They must have enlarged in a matter of hours. I palpated them with disgust, in their closed shell they concealed the living evidence of a lethal disturbance. They were the obscene sign that something in Jean's body was endeavouring to bring about his downfall. A thing – virus, bacterium, germ – was proliferating in his organs. His beard was constantly wet with sweat. His fever was tenacious. I did not allow myself any respite. I scarcely dozed for a few hours, curled up in a ball at the foot of his bed like a miserable dog. I tried to find out the cause of his illness, went over in detail what he'd eaten in the past few days, came up with nothing that could have caused food poisoning. I felt his head, checked his old injuries. Nothing. I opened his mouth, searched it with a flashlight. The back of his throat seemed irritated. His tongue was whitish. I palpated his stomach. I imagined him infested with worms or that during the night a rat had managed to lodge in his intestines. Impossible, but I thought it, and that was enough to drive me to despair.

It had never occurred to me that Jean might die. That fear may have been justified when I brought him home. He had shown then so few signs of life that I should have expected the worst. But no. As if his death had no meaning. I could not comprehend the blind force that had inhabited me once I'd understood that Jean was not only part of my life but that he *was* my life. That assurance now had left me. Jean was going to die unless I found out how to heal him.

Then an insidious thought found its way to my heart. Jean's malady was her. My mother.

She hadn't liked my getting rid of her belongings, hadn't tolerated the sight of her son just tossing the remains of her deceased life into garbage bags. She knew everything, saw everything, attacked, undermined that which I loved. Nothing better than death to look down on the everyday life of the living. Sublime place. No one can dislodge you from it. She had spied on me from the beginning of her end.

She had died in order to see, finally, what sort of son I was.

THE PHOTO

After sitting up three nights with Jean, hopeless, I went down to the cellar. It was barely dawn. I was staggering with fatigue. I'd decided to put back in place everything that had belonged to my mother. I was ready for that act of cowardice. I would return her clothes to their drawers, restock her medicine chest with her old cosmetics, put the magnetized animals back on the fridge. Everything would be as it was before. And if I had to, I would go to the town dump to find the two garbage bags already taken away!

I had abdicated. Dead, she seemed to me more powerful than alive, having all the time she wanted to do me harm. The house disgusted me, as if my mother's corpse were rotting inside its walls, contaminated by her unhealthy desire for her husband.

I was standing in front of the pile of garbage bags as if Jean's disease – cancer – were spread in front of me. In the dirty darkness of the cellar they breathed like so many black, foul-smelling lungs. Bending over to pick one up I sensed the presence of my mother. Turning around, I noticed the big photo from her fortieth birthday. Though I thought I'd stowed it in an old cardboard box. Obviously I hadn't done what I'd intended: I'd simply put it in the box. I understood why I couldn't tolerate that photo very long when it had pride of place in the living room. My mother, in her spotless nurse's uniform, displaying her benevolent cruelty. Her real face appeared. An expression of hatred. Hard. Intransigent. The face of a murderer.

"You have no power, Mama, no rights. You can't see me. You've seen nothing. You don't know that Jean is living in your bed. You know nothing because you are nothing."

I smashed the picture while I looked, disgusted, at the garbage bags: my mother's things would sit there and rot. While I was going up the cellar stairs, the name of Josiane Gravel rang out in my head. I went to call her. She was a professional nurse. She would know what to do for Jean.

I spent one whole day hesitating by the telephone. How to persuade her to come to my place? To say what? Would she laugh in my face? Inviting Josiane Gravel struck me now as unthinkable, even dangerous. As for asking a doctor for help or calling an ambulance, that was out of the question. I wasn't crazy. No one would understand. They would take Jean away from me. Put me in jail. And without me, Jean would die.

THE CAKE

Jean's condition was worsening by the hour. No way to make him swallow water. His reflexes had deserted him. I could barely make out the sound of his breathing. After two more days of hesitation I made my decision: I would call Josiane.

I needed a pretext. I got the idea of making her think it was my birthday, which wasn't true because I'd turned thirty-seven three months earlier. While we were eating, I would inform her that someone had rented my mother's room. I would tell her about him: a fine man. He'd have loved to join us for this birthday meal but he had suddenly taken sick ... No, no, nothing serious, but I'm concerned all the same ... Could she look at him? Yes, he had a slight fever ... Could she tell me what she thought? She had been so professional, so competent when caring for my mother ...

Holding my breath, I called her. Two minutes later I was on my knees in the living room, thanking God. Josiane, in a muffled voice, had simply said she'd come.

She didn't seem surprised, didn't ask questions, didn't refer to the memory of my mother. Nothing. As if we'd seen each other only the day before. She didn't even mention the notebooks. Not the slightest hint. A miracle.

I showered, shaved, shopped. I bought a barbecued chicken, a bottle of wine, and a cake on which I'd had written *Happy Birthday Edgar*.

I was expecting her around seven o'clock. She knocked on my door precisely at seven o'clock. From the window where I'd been watching for her I hadn't seen a car. I concluded that she'd taken the bus. She must have walked for a good ten minutes after she got off. When she was looking after my mother she would take a taxi and get reimbursed. I showed her in. A moment's silence. Short, but heavy enough to make us both freeze. She took off her hat. An ugly tuque. Her hair was black, she'd stopped bleaching it. She shed her coat, asked if she should take off her boots, which were dripping with dirty snow. I said it wasn't necessary. She seemed surprised but finally smiled faintly. She opened her purse and took out a small package wrapped in tissue paper. I put coat, tuque, and purse in the closet by the front door. Realized my hands were trembling. When I came back she wished me Happy Birthday and handed me a present, blushing. I opened it. A necktie, apple green. I wanted to slap her. And immediately afterwards, to take her in my arms, to melt into hers.

A necktie.

The gift took away all modesty. I had to act quickly. I seated Josiane at the already-set table. Salad, chicken, cake, wine. Josiane pointed out that the house seemed bigger. The wine was terrible. Josiane did not complain. She was polite. I kept waiting for her to bring up the notebooks. She was no doubt waiting for me to ask about her fiancé or her wedding. I was sure there had never been either fiancé or wedding. She had lied to me. Otherwise, what was she doing here? She definitely wanted something. I watched her eat the chicken. Her dark hair – she was no longer bottle blonde – made her look more determined. Strangely, it made her look younger. I could imagine her as the child she had been. No doubt unhappy as a teen. A tormented being. Like me. I was wrong: she wasn't ugly. Or beautiful. Or pretty. Or anything. Ordinary, watered-down, uninteresting. Like me. Basically, she looked like me.

The chicken finished, she brought up the notebooks. Had I understood her intentions? I watched her delicate hands. She had on a sweater that made her look fat. I took away the plates, came back from the kitchen with the cake. I felt like an idiot, I'd gone to the trouble of planting thirty-seven candles in it. All at once I found this farce embarrassing, heavy-handed. What would she think about a man who decorated his own birthday cake? Finally I told her about my tenant. I babbled a little but I stuck to my scenario. She showed no sign of surprise or annoyance, as if the unexpected had no hold on her. I even felt the diversion came as a relief. The atmosphere during the meal had been heavy. She had anticipated something else from me. More attentiveness? More curiosity about her? After all, if I had invited her, alone, to this bogus birthday, given the circumstances that had put us back in touch she was entitled to hope for something better than my sluggish presence. I felt no desire for her.

She followed me up the stairs.

When I showed her into the bedroom she immediately brought her hand to her mouth. Then stepped back as if she were going to vomit. I realized how accustomed I'd become to the stench inside these walls. Jean was decomposing. Or some unknown thing was rotting inside him. Josiane looked at me, incredulous. I pushed her towards the bed. Nothing happened as I had hoped it would. Jean, with his dirty hair and unkempt beard, did not correspond with the reserved and dependable tenant I'd just described. Instead, he called to mind some dying vermin, a nightmare creature. She took his pulse, that's all she did, then rushed out of the room.

Had Josiane come too late? I went downstairs to join her. She was in the living room, dialing a number. I grabbed the phone from her.

What happened after that? No matter how I search my memory I can't reconstitute exactly how events unfurled. There is still a hole where today again I am drowning. I killed her, that's my only certainty. I killed Josiane Gravel by stabbing her with a knife. Repeatedly. I imagine she tried to convince me it was extremely urgent to ask for help. Had she realized something was wrong on entering the bedroom? Her nurse's instinct, I assume. She was afraid. For herself. For the unknown man rotting away upstairs. Was she calling an ambulance or the police? I'll never know. I remember I looked at my birthday cake. I was yelling, I think, that one mustn't be taken in by appearances. If anyone could help me it was her, her and no one else! Did I tell her that the unknown man's name was Jean? Did I repeat that there was no question of telling anyone at all? Did I beg her to go back upstairs and do everything she could to save him? With what words? I don't remember. What did she say? What did she do? I don't remember that either. I looked at the birthday cake sitting on the small table in the living room, that's all I remember. And also the knife I would have cut it with if everything had happened as I'd naively hoped, that I had used instead for bringing the life of Josiane Gravel to an end.

THE ARROW

I was surprised – not stunned, but surprised – that everything happened as in detective films or novels. Killing someone wasn't hard. It happened. Fast. Very fast. Especially since it wasn't planned.

I took Josiane Gravel's body down to the cellar. I don't think I imagined getting rid of it any other way. For lack of money, I'd never finished renovating it. The floor was beaten earth, so I only had to shift the garbage bags, dig a hole, bury Josiane Gravel, put back the bags. I also buried her coat, her tuque, her purse, the necktie in its giftwrap, and the knife.

The digging had worn me out. Back in the living room the thought that Jean might be dead passed through my heart. Should I have waited before filling in the hole in the cellar? Hearing myself formulate the question plunged me into deep despair. I'd reached that point: I was concerned about that kind of detail even though I could not imagine life after Jean. Nauseated, I lay down on the living-room sofa, not daring to go back upstairs. I disappeared into a sticky sleep. The arrow. It was hounding me again. This time I caught sight of the man who'd shot it. He was walking towards me, carrying a crossbow. I fled as fast as my legs would carry me, trying to avoid obstacles, trees that abruptly emerged from the earth along the way. Out of breath, on my knees, I felt the back of my neck crack on impact. I opened my eyes, there was someone in the living room. I could make out in the half-light the scrawny silhouette of a creature from beyond the grave. The man with the crossbow, out of my dream, approached me. It was Jean.

His naked body, startlingly thin, intimidated me. I had the impression I was studying an object I didn't know how to use. I said his name, he didn't flinch. I touched his shoulder, he moved his lips. I made him sit down and gave him some water. He still had a fever, but since he'd been able to get up, go down the stairs, how could I not hope the worst was over? He was going to live, I should never have had any doubt. What a son of a bitch I'd been! It was a big mistake to have invited Josiane Gravel, I realized that painfully now.

I settled Jean in my bed; too many toxic odours haunted his room. The next day I disinfected it completely. I washed everything: sheets, curtains, walls, floor. Despite the cold I opened the window. The icy air drove away the last remnants of sickness. Towards the beginning of the evening I returned Jean to his room. His lymph nodes had pretty well shrunk. He had eaten a bit of puréed vegetables. I myself hadn't eaten anything since the day before. I opened a can of soup, gulped it down with a piece of bread. I got my birthday cake, which I'd left in the living room, and set it in the middle of the kitchen table. I looked at the letters written in red on the icing and felt an urge to cry like a child: *Happy Birthday Edgar.*

I had become a murderer.

I lit the thirty-seven candles, asked God's forgiveness for my sins, and vowed to devote myself to his living son. I blew out the candles and cut myself a piece. I was just about to eat it when I heard an unusual sound. I paid close attention, recognizing the first notes of "À la claire fontaine." The melody seemed to be coming from very far away. Then it stopped suddenly. I put down my fork and looked around me. The little radio on the kitchen counter was turned off. I checked the TV. Off as well. Again, the same notes, which soon stopped. I opened the cellar door, went down the stairs. The melody rose again from the pile of garbage bags, like a muffled lament, a distant song that calmed my heart. No, it was not the ghost of Josiane Gravel here to sing "À la claire fontaine." It was her phone.

It kept ringing all evening, to midnight and beyond. Someone was looking for her. It was clear that her absence had been reported. I imagined the whole city already looking for her. The next day, late in the afternoon, the ringing stopped. The phone battery had given up the ghost. It was time, I was about to dig up Josiane Gravel.

I dumped the cake and its thirty-seven pathetic candles without tasting it.

THE INSPECTORS

I dared not leave the house now, I was afraid of breaking into "À la claire fontaine" at the top of my lungs in front of astonished passersby. I, Edgar Trudel, had killed someone. I banged my head against my bedroom wall.

One night I retreated to Jean's bed and snuggled up against him. It was the first time I'd ever put my arms around someone. I was surprised that a body could be so warm, that mine could enjoy it so eagerly.

I had decided to chain him up only when I had to leave the house. Occasionally when I was there, he would take a few steps, then come to a halt, waiting for me to go to him. I detected a glimmer of relief in his eyes when I helped him sit in an armchair. I did not understand how that evening he'd been able to come down the stairs by himself. As if the death of Josiane Gravel had made possible Jean's recovery, as if communicating vessels had linked their existences. Despite that comforting idea I spent my days saying one Our Father after another. I needed that to chase away my acute fear: what if the police tracked me down? Josiane Gravel had written to me, I'd written to her, and we had talked on the phone. It would be easy to establish a connection between us.

During my fake birthday meal I had convinced myself that she lived alone. Now I was not so sure. I had called her only once and she'd answered right away. From that I'd concluded she lived alone. How naive! Her husband could have been holding her in his arms while she spoke with me. How to be absolutely sure that she hadn't told someone about our plan to meet? As the days went by I kept turning over different scenarios that all arrived at this conclusion: someone in Josiane Gravel's circle knew something. Her fiancé or her husband, her mother, her sister, a neighbour?

In the throes of unbearable anxiety, I switched on the TV. I couldn't have done it earlier. I hadn't read a newspaper or even listened to the radio for a month. Two or three times I had gone out to shop, that was all. I was expecting that at any moment the house would be surrounded by armed police. In fact, I hoped so. Why, after so many endless days, had no one come to arrest me? I wanted to know who had called Josiane Gravel and rehearsed in my head dozens of times, "Il y a long-temps que je t'aime," words that every day came back to haunt me. I wanted to know if it was him, her fiancé, her husband, we would see on TV reports begging the population to find his beloved. I wanted to know who it was that I had really killed.

I zapped several times before I came on the end of a report that attracted my attention. It was not about the disappearance of Josiane Gravel but rather the murder of a singer. Her murderer had been on the run after months of investigation. The report ended with her photo and her name: Émilie Langevin (1980–2001). I zapped again but found nothing about Josiane Gravel. Finally I decided to go out and buy the papers. It was snowing heavily. I donned boots and coat. Just as I was about to leave, there was a knock at the door. Since my mother's death no one had knocked on that door except Josiane Gravel.

It was them. They'd found me. They were coming to arrest me.

I opened the door. Two men asked me if I was Edgar Trudel. I stammered something. They were indeed two police inspectors. They were investigating the disappearance of Josiane Gravel. They knew I'd called her the day before she disappeared. The record of her telephone calls showed it beyond the shadow of a doubt. I invited them to sit down at the kitchen table, offered them coffee. They said no, asked if I lived alone. I replied that since my mother's death that was the case. The question had upset me intensely. Jean had to stay silent now, I thought. What would I have told them if he'd come downstairs and shown himself to them, naked or decked out in a diaper? Happily nothing of the sort happened. I explained to the two inspectors that Josiane Gravel had taken care of my mother. I had barely known her, only enough to appreciate her merits, especially her professional skills. In fact, I had practically forgotten her existence but the anniversary of my mother's death had brought her back to mind. I had recently called then to thank her and see how she was doing. It was strictly polite, nothing more.

No, Josiane Gravel had mentioned nothing out of the ordinary when we spoke. No, I had no idea where she might be found. No, I knew nothing about her private life. Yes, I was affected by her disappearance.

They apologized politely for taking up my time, gave me a phone number to reach them in case I found out anything new. "You never know," said the one who'd asked most of the questions. The other was taking notes on a small pad. Throughout the interrogation I had kept my coat on. My shirt was soaked in sweat.

With the inspectors gone, I felt sure of one thing: Josiane Gravel had told no one she was coming to my house or the two cops would have shown it in one way or another. She had never had a fiancé. It was her mother or a friend who had called her shortly after she disappeared. In any case I would never know, with the record of the earlier phone call hidden in the electronic guts of her telephone, near her corpse. She had accepted my invitation because she'd hoped for something from our being together. Her expectations had been largely unfounded.

I hadn't gone out to buy the papers. The following day the name of Émilie Langevin, the murdered singer, again caught my attention. It reminded me of someone or something though I couldn't connect it with a specific event. Often in the course of the day the singer's name came back and haunted me like a small wound that reminds the body of its presence. Then the inspectors' visit had made me agitated. I jumped at the slightest sound, positioned myself behind the living-room window watching for I don't know whom, observing every car that drove by. I no longer felt certain that I'd convinced the two inspectors. I had kept my coat on all the time they were questioning me – carelessness on my part. Why hadn't I taken it off? I had something to hide, that was clear. As usual, I kept turning over hypotheses in my mind, reasoning that ultimately shed no light on anything.

One of the two inspectors, the one with the notepad, called me a few weeks later. No, I had nothing new for him. Josiane Gravel was still an unsolved case, like so many others here, he told me.

Many times I thought I heard the obsessive melody of Josiane's telephone ringing up from the cellar. I suffered from auditory hallucinations, affected by the overly long months of winter now that I had chosen to live practically as a shutaway. I had grown thin while Jean now sported a slight layer of fat. His face had regained its childish plumpness. He seemed happy, was so obedient he moved me to tears. He now spoke a few words: *sit, lie down, open your mouth* … I slept with him more often. He rarely got up on his own, waiting for me to say *get up* before doing so. He had stopped moaning and complaining. His green eyes were no longer empty, something alarming came up to their surface: the icy tip of a desire.

Spring arrived. I was not the kind who went into ecstasies over the end of winter but this time, the melting of the snow had a beneficial effect on me. My nervous system was no longer in desperate straits, it was as if I'd been able to turn a painful page.

One incident however put an end to that brief lull. I was on the main floor putting away the lunch dishes when I heard an unusual sound, a kind of long, shrill lament, nearly like a baby's moaning. I rushed upstairs, went into Jean's room. He was holding a cat in his hands. The animal must have come in the window that I'd left ajar that morning. Very quickly I realized that something was up. Jean's expression was one I'd never seen. A kind of astonished pleasure. And the cat was dangling in his hands like something soft. I wanted to take it but Jean pushed me away. I hit him and took the cat. Its dead body was still warm. I stuffed it into a plastic bag and went down to throw it in the garbage.

It was a pure black little cat, definitely not the one that had jumped in my face. That one must have been huge.

"À la claire fontaine, un ange vint dormir."

Shortly afterwards I woke up with that phrase in my head. Over the following days I couldn't get rid of it. It had become embedded in my mind, spinning non-stop like a demented top: "By the clear fountain, an angel came to sleep … an angel came … an angel came to sleep …" The demented notion that I was Jean's assailant had resurfaced, hooked onto that obsessive phrase like some ridiculous little bell. The more I reasoned with myself, the more I blamed myself: I had noticed him at the graveyard in his red dress. I had guessed at first glance that it was a man, it was so obvious: the broad shoulders, the muscular legs. I had imagined the story of the Four Horsemen of the Apocalypse. Why horsemen, why the Apocalypse?

I had imagined the whole story so as not to see what I had done.

THE FRIDGE

Change the rhythm of my days, find other activities –
that's what would help rid me of my obsessions. The April
sun was shining behind the grimy windows of the house.
I set out to do some spring cleaning: shake the carpets,
wash the curtains, rid the ceilings of their cobwebs, paint.

I started by opening all the windows. Fresh air
circulated through the rooms, stirring the curtains,
driving out the dust. Before long the strong odour of
damp earth came into the house. I had settled Jean on
the ground floor. From the living-room sofa, he was
listening to the deafening song of the sparrows. I had
dressed him in old clothes of mine, a pair of jeans and
a white T-shirt.

Where to begin? Rugs, windows, fridge? It hadn't
been cleaned for several years. I unplugged it, emptied it
completely. Lots of food, forgotten in various compart-
ments, was covered with mould. I filled a garbage can
with jars of uncertain contents. I took a break, long
enough for the freezer compartment to thaw, and went
to see Jean in the living room. He hadn't moved. I told
him, "Up." He stood and opened his mouth. It was well
past time for his noon meal, he was expecting that
I would feed him. A squirrel climbed onto the window
ledge. It was nibbling on a piece of apple it must have
found in a garbage can. Jean took a step towards it. The
squirrel froze. Jean took another step. With one leap

the squirrel ran away. A click was heard: "À la claire fontaine, un ange vint dormir." I had just understood the reason for my obsession!

I took Jean back to his room. After closing all the windows I left the house, started the car, and went to the cemetery. To find what I was looking for I first had to go to my mother's grave, even though I'd sworn never again to set foot there.

The afternoon sun was shining high in the sky, and despite the tombstones, no sorrow could spoil the bright clarity of the day. The cemetery had the appearance of a vast sea of graves with crosses and angels' heads emerging from it. People circulated among the graves, placing flowers at the headstones. Some had brought supplies for cleaning their family chapel. The first sunny day of spring had given a good many people an urge to do spring cleaning.

Planted in front of the small slab of marble where her first name and my father's surname sparkled – ANNE-MARIE TRUDEL – I reconstructed events: I'd fallen asleep on my mother's grave, cries had wakened me, I had climbed a small mound where I'd spotted the Four Horsemen of the Apocalypse. That was on a rainy autumn night. All that had really existed, I hadn't imagined it. After several attempts I spotted the grave I was looking for. That night, as I approached the site of the attack, a sound made me turn my head. A squirrel that was gnawing at a pine cone on the closest grave fled at once. That was when I'd read unconsciously the inscription carved into the stone: ÉMILIE LANGEVIN 1980–2001. The squirrel I'd noticed a while before, that Jean had approached, had unlocked my memory with its leap.

Émilie Langevin … *l'ange vint* … the angel came … a murdered singer …

I had thought that the angel in the phrase was the accusatory ghost of the woman I had buried in the cellar. It seemed obvious to me. I was totally wrong. Josiane Gravel was not the angel I was obsessed with. It was the murdered singer, Émilie Langevin. And I now knew where I had seen her name: on the grave where Jean was attacked.

I didn't go back to the house right away; I needed time to think. I drove across town, parked not far from the port. I made my way to a landscaped plaza that ran along the St. Lawrence, I needed space too. I spent a long moment sitting on a bench. I gazed at the gulls wheeling in the sky or touching down near the public garbage bins. It was very windy. Despite the brutality of the sunlight that wasn't letting up, I was freezing with my arms wrapped around my belly and it had brought me to a standstill. There were thousands of graves in the cemetery, the largest in the city, maybe in the whole country. That grave or another, what was the difference? Yet I couldn't convince myself that there was no connection between Jean and Émilie Langevin, both of them victims of assaults. One had been murdered, I had saved the other. What event exactly had I witnessed that night?

I had to go home, Jean had eaten practically nothing all day. Seated in the car, I changed my mind, drove downtown, and went into a record store. I asked a salesman if he knew a singer named Émilie Langevin. He said no. Somewhat relieved by his answer I decided it was best to drop that story.

Back at the house, my priority was to deal with the fridge. The freezer section was completely thawed, creating a puddle of dirty water on the floor. I cleaned the kitchen, put whatever was still edible back in the fridge. The day was drawing to an end. Spring cleaning would wait for another day. I fixed a bowl of cereal for Jean, got him to eat it while I made do with two dry biscuits.

I couldn't help it, the next day I went into a bookstore a few minutes from the house. There were books for sale and also records and kitschy doodads. I searched the racks, unsuccessfully. Nothing in the *L* section was even close to *Langevin*. I asked the young girl behind the counter. The name Émilie Langevin reminded her vaguely of something. I told her the singer had been murdered. Her face lit up. She disappeared behind some shelves and came back with a CD. I bought it.

Émilie Langevin had been part of the group Fatal Foetus. I knew nothing about Goth metal. A leaflet inside the jewel case traced a brief history of that musical style born in the early 1990s. I didn't learn much: murky atmosphere, self-destructive behaviour, a female voice integrated into a world of cold, metallic sounds. I listened for a few minutes. That was enough. The CD cover in particular bothered me: four women dressed in black surrounded another wearing a long coat partly open to her bare stomach: Émilie Langevin. All five women had long, black hair. And black lines painted around their eyes.

Fatal Foetus: the name upset me as much as the titles of their songs, more or less perverse, sometimes incomprehensible. I threw the CD in the garbage and lost myself in my spring cleaning, this time swearing not to think about all that.

THE WIG

The list of instructions to which Jean responded was getting longer every day. I would tell him "Eat," he ate. Without my orders he was passive: "Dress, lie down, sit down." Life was getting easier. He had gained weight and spent less time sleeping. The scorching heat of summer nights was here. It made for difficulty sleeping. The humidity in the city and its polluted air weighed down on us by day. I would have liked to take Jean to a park or have him sit on the small front lawn, in the shadow of the old oak tree. I dared not do so, no one must suspect that he was staying with me. Jean was condemned to stay hidden, I did not see how things could have worked out otherwise.

I abided by his tastes, ate what he liked to eat, especially meat. There were times when I contented myself with anything he'd left on his plate. I needed to feel smaller than him and tried hard to find anything that would humble me. For every order I gave him I wished I could hurt myself, a matter of compensating. But I resisted that temptation, which would have led to disaster. Also, well, I came to accept that Jean obeyed me like a little animal. I had to assume the distinctive characteristic of our relationship. He wore my clothes, I washed in his bathwater. He guessed what I thought and I thought what he guessed.

Following my cleaning frenzy, I had developed an uncontrollable passion for housework, to which I now devoted a large part of my time. I was constantly discovering dirt; you'd think it was born of a minor negligence, an absence of a few hours, a momentary lapse in concentration. I washed the bathroom every day, dusted the lampshades every week, even cleaned the light bulbs. I started to clean the layer of grime from inside the kitchen drawers. I unearthed remains of food, dried-up insects, even the mummified corpse of a mouse. I spent hours cleaning the storage space under the sink. I was sleeping better. Summer had ended without incident. Nothing from the police inspectors. No one had rung my doorbell to question me about Josiane Gravel. No one had noticed her at my place. If only it could continue.

I was delighted at the physical change in Jean, at how quickly his cheeks, belly, buttocks had lost their emaciated look. I had to buy clothes for him, mine no longer fit. Despite all this surprising progress I still had to diaper him. One day as I was storing some in the chest of drawers, I came across the wig that I'd taken for an animal. It was still in its plastic bag, hidden under some sheets. I went to the bathroom, stood at the mirror, tried it on.

"Hello. What's your name?"

"It's a secret."

"How are you today?"

"I'm very well. Why?"

"Because life is beautiful. Thanks for your reply. I couldn't imagine one more true. Do you love someone?"

"I don't want to answer that."

"It's clear that you love someone. But look at yourself."

"What?"

"Your face."

My face.

Was it my mother's face that I'd just recognized in the mirror? I took off the wig, went downstairs to throw it in the garbage. Just as I was about to do so I noticed a small label sewn onto the back of the wig. On it two words were written in purple ink: *Fatal Foetus*. I felt as if I were holding in my hand a slimy animal, eyeless but omniscient, ready to bite my head and absorb everything that was swarming inside it.

THE CORPORAL

I went out to buy the Fatal Foetus record. I studied more closely the photo on the CD jewel case: all five members of the group wore wigs identical to the one I had in my possession. Beyond any doubt, there was a link between Jean and Émilie Langevin. The worm had reached the core of the apple. I already knew too much – and at the same time, too little. The discovery had just caused the dikes of my protection system to give way, though until now they had kept Jean and me in perfect symbiosis.

I went to the municipal library where after a quick search I found an article mentioning that Émilie Langevin had been murdered in September two years earlier. I concentrated on that period. With a few clicks, information was piling up: Émilie Langevin had had her vagina and her anus torn, probably by a knife, and she was missing an eye. She had bled to death. Corporal Alex Lévis, her ex-fiancé, had been suspected of murder but no proof could be established and he'd been released after a few days. One year earlier, Alex Lévis had come back highly disturbed from Kosovo, where he'd served with NATO forces. When he returned, Émilie Langevin had let him know that their love affair was no longer possible. Her singing career had taken off and occupied all her time. The corporal had made some vague threats before he disappeared from her life.

Scouring the most recent papers I came across a series of articles reporting on the disappearance of Corporal Alex Lévis. There were several references to a possible suicide. One article put forward, with no clue to justify such a hypothesis, that he had jumped into the St. Lawrence. And then I had before my eyes a photo of the corporal: it was Jean.

I left the library, livid. I walked for hours, circling the same streets. The dozen or so articles I'd just read onscreen created a persistent fog inside my head. Evening arrived. I went into a bar full of students newly back from vacation. You could tell they were students simply by their tans, their excitement at being together in a flock. I ordered a beer, then another and another. I hated the taste but I could have gone on drinking all night, surrounded by these young people crammed full of future, engulfed by the pulse of their carefree bodies. Aided by alcohol, I saw again the Four Horsemen of the Apocalypse emerge from the night; fiercely and relentlessly, they went at the man whose identity I had learned that night. Something was wrong. Angels dispensing justice, not at all apocalyptic, that's what they had been. I had witnessed a scene of revenge: those four men had beaten up Corporal Alex Lévis to take revenge for the murder of Émilie Langevin. For them, he was the singer's murderer beyond the shadow of a doubt.

But who were those four men?

A flash of inspiration shot through me. They were not men whom I'd spotted in the dim light of the cemetery, they were women: the members of Fatal Foetus! Like an obsessed police officer, I pieced together the thread of events, went over the scenes, went back to the events, alcohol creating in my mind the sordid details: four female musicians, wearing military uniforms, kidnap the corporal, threatening him with a revolver. They undress him, tie him up, paint his face outrageously, make him don the dress and wig worn by Émilie Langevin, lock him in the trunk of a car, and drive to the cemetery.

If I hadn't fallen asleep I would have witnessed it all: the corporal being dragged to Émilie Langevin's grave, humiliated, soiled, skewered to the depths of his soul so that he would live the horror of the rape he had made his victim suffer – and to finish, trampled with their boots and left for dead, hoping that the ghost of the Fatal Foetus singer had enjoyed the show.

I left the bar, reeling. I was drunk for the first time in my life. In the car I added the finishing touches to the degrading acts the man I was about to see at home had been subjected to. The condom, yes, to humiliate him they must have stuffed it down his throat with the branch. No limit to revenge! Let him croak, that rapist, that sadist! He made me puke.

I parked under the oak tree, exasperated at not having the courage to drive right into the lugubrious mass of its trunk. Before I went inside, I vomited. Disgusted, I opened the door. Jean stood there facing me. He had broken his chain. Émilie Langevin's murderer was smiling.

He terrified me.

I took refuge in my room. My head was spinning. I got into bed with all my clothes on and fell asleep before my eyes were shut.

Rain that fell on the roof like knives woke me up. I went to the window. The street was transformed into a nervous stream rushing towards the city centre. I still had the taste of vomit in my mouth and my head was torturing me. I went to the bathroom to freshen up. There was blood in the sink. I realized there was some on the floor as well. I left the room and went downstairs where a trail of blood led me to the living room.

Jean was on his knees, blood was trickling down his arms and legs, dripping onto the carpet where it traced new patterns. I froze, looked at him, not understanding.

"Edgar! Edgar!"

Someone was calling me by name. I turned around but saw no one.

"Edgar! Edgar!"

I heard my name again: Jean was calling me. For the first time I was hearing his voice. It was inside me, reverberating in the bones of my skull. He had searched in my memory, found the way to my scars, now was offering me his wounds to care for mine. He spread his arms and I took refuge there.

The rain was pelting down, so hard, the house seemed so vulnerable ... Yet I felt a new force, immense, as I shivered in his arms. He knew everything. I had doubted him, he appeased my soul with the revelation of his innocence. He had done it with the only means available: his blood. I was angry with myself, I who was supposed to protect him, I too had fallen into the trap. Jean was a lamb, not a hangman. A helpless child in an adult body.

Obviously everything was against him. He was the ideal suspect and for that very reason, he should *not* be the guilty party. I understood what had happened: he had been taken in.

The truth was hidden in the dark, disgusting songs of Fatal Foetus, which were about bestiality, vile rituals, all coated with squawking, aggressive music. Besides, the group's name was evocative. What did it mean if not that its musicians carried within themselves the seed of evil? Émilie Langevin had been killed during an orgy gone bad. And who knows if she had provoked her horrible end herself? Jean had unmasked the four musicians and was preparing to denounce them. They'd gone into action by simulating an act of revenge to be certain that he would be considered guilty definitively. It was so obvious!

The months that followed were the happiest of my life. Freed from myself, I now devoted myself entirely to Jean's welfare. He was my child and for brief moments, curled up in his arms, I became his.

THE JEWEL BOX

I had just one worry: money. My mother's inheritance had nearly run out, I could no longer pay my bills. Winter was nigh, heating was expensive. Jean's appetite continued to grow. Sooner or later I would have to resign myself to getting a job. I found it hard to imagine leaving Jean alone in the house all day. Some mornings I got up with the thought of buying lottery tickets. I dreamed without believing in it about bank robberies. I was reduced to picking up supermarket flyers and noting what products were featured that week! The slightest saving constituted a small victory. In this way I came across a leaflet from a drugstore chain that had an ad for adult diapers. The product was definitely becoming increasingly popular. To my great shame I promptly got into the car so as not to miss that rare opportunity. I bought a good supply of diapers. In the line where I was awaiting my turn to pay my eyes were drawn to the front page of a big daily displayed on a rack. Large letters read: AN EYE IN HER FREEZER.

A photo accompanied the sensational headline: a woman with one foot in her house, the other on her balcony. She'd gone outside in a dressing gown to get away from journalists or to answer their questions, who knows? In the photo she looked distraught. Under it, I read: "Yesterday morning, Madame Lévis found a human eye in her freezer."

I picked up a copy of the paper, went to the cash with my diapers, paid, and fled as though I were the monster who had cut out the eye.

In the days that followed I bought different papers to follow the story in all its detail. I even switched on the TV, something I'd rarely done since I'd murdered Josiane. It was official, there'd been tests, the eye was that of Émilie Langevin. The missing piece had been found. Madame Lévis had had the surprise of her life when she discovered it in a small box where she usually stored her ring. She explained to the police that she didn't know exactly when her son could have hidden it in the freezer. It could have been there for more than two years. When he returned from Kosovo, traumatized, Corporal Alex Lévis had come back to live with her for a while, then disappeared without leaving an address. Her husband having died some ten years earlier, she had lived alone since then, working in a small grooming parlour for dogs of which she was co-owner. She had nothing else to disclose.

Why had the corporal killed and put out the eye of his former fiancée? Why had he kept that eye? And what was it doing in his mother's freezer? In the papers, those questions were displayed in bold type.

The plot was thickening. People were hounding Jean again. It was practical to accuse someone thought to have committed suicide, someone believed to be rotting away at the bottom of a river. Most important, they wanted to close the file once and for all. I was the only person who knew what the members of Fatal Foetus had inflicted on Jean. There was no doubt in my mind: those four women had managed to conceal the eye in the freezer of the corporal's mother. I was haunted by the thought of writing an anonymous letter to the police to denounce them, but it was too risky. In any case I couldn't have provided any evidence without unmasking myself. It was better if I too were to file away the question of Émilie Langevin.

During the week when these slanderous revelations were on the rise, a newspaper published another photo of Madame Lévis. This time she was shown in front of her workplace. She had the same distraught look. On her left was the sign of her business, Cuddle Pups. On her right, in the display window partially hidden by her, a placard. Help Wanted immediately drew my attention. I turned towards Jean, who was eating, and to my own astonishment, told him I would soon be working for his mama. I had the feeling then that he had grasped perfectly what I'd just told him.

I found the address of Cuddle Pups in the Yellow Pages. I had no experience in dog grooming. I had no idea such services were even available. Without being able to explain it, though, I was convinced that I would get the job, that from now on Jean and I would be able to survive thanks to his mother's money and my own innate skill at grooming dogs.

DOGS

The room that served as an office for Madame Lévis had fluorescent lights; its walls were covered with photos glorifying the canine world; and the office smelled musty and sweaty. Jean's mother still had the distraught expression I had seen in her photos, as if anguish had carved the bones of her face. The luminous green of her eyes, similar to her son's, struck me immediately. When I telephoned, I had been surprised that she welcomed me readily despite the circumstances surrounding the accusations focused on her son, suggesting we meet the next day. I thought she was quite warm. No doubt more so with strangers than with family and friends. I would like to have asked why she had alerted the police, why she had not simply thrown the eye in the toilet. She knew perfectly well that this discovery would incriminate her son. I would never understand how mothers operate. Maybe she wanted to finish this business once and for all. Make a clean sweep. Do her duty. Expose the monster to whom she thought she'd given birth, to cleanse her belly for good. After all, my own mother had practically drowned me.

Madame Lévis talked to me at length about her love of animals, the only love, according to her, that was unconditional. And it was in her stifling little office that I realized Jean had had the bad luck not to be born a dog. It was while listening to her talk about endangered species, about injustice towards animals, about their rights being scoffed at, about man's wickedness towards them, about the shameless and boundless exploitation of which they were victims, that I swore to myself I would be the mother Jean had never had.

Overnight, I had a job, a salary. Madame Lévis hired me on a trial basis for two months. I was trained by her co-owner, Madame Bellavance. She showed me how to behave with the dogs, explained how to use products designed especially for them, listed the various treatments available. A week later, I had done my first grooming, and the week after that, my first clipping – a poodle. At first Madame Bellavance was skeptical about me. I did not match the usual profile. It was mainly a job for young students. I behaved with her like a servile student, very attentive. As she liked people weaker than herself and couldn't stand being contradicted, I went out of my way to play the idiot. I wanted at all costs to keep this job and so I went out of the way to go along with her whims and her mood swings. She seemed younger than me but I was sure she was a few years older. Her distrust disappeared quickly. Barely a month after I was hired, she complimented me on my work in front of Madame Lévis. She thought I was talented, going so far as to say that I maintained a genuine relationship with the dogs. It was true, I felt comfortable with them, large or small, docile or stubborn.

Cuddle Pups was located in the far east of the city. It took nearly half an hour to get there. I left at eight in the morning and did not come home until six at night. There was no question of going home to fix Jean his noon meal. I had to improvise. I obtained a collar and a long metal chain, stronger than the earlier one, to tie him up in such a way that he couldn't get far from his bed. Before I left for work I arranged large quantities of food and water on his bedroom floor. Saturdays, I was so exhausted I slept a good part of the day. After a few months I found my rhythm. Jean however was less obedient since I'd been working. He felt neglected. I understood his change in attitude but I had no choice.

He gained weight with amazing speed, which caused problems for my washing him, especially when he insisted on staying in bed for days at a time. I could no longer lift him. I decided to put him on a diet, gradually reducing the amount of food I set down on the floor. I went to work one morning leaving him just a bowl of water and a little rice. On my return, an unusually violent smell of excrement greeted me. I went upstairs. Jean had torn his sheets, knocked over the furniture he'd been able to reach, broken what he couldn't. He had cut himself on shards of the ceramic lamp sitting on the chest of drawers. His shit, his piss, his blood covered the walls, the remnants. Seeing me, he started to laugh. I had never seen Jean laugh.

The next day I called in to work to say I was sick, cleaned and repaired as much as possible, emptied the fridge, and brought everything it contained up to the bedroom. Jean gulped it all down without taking time to catch his breath. There was such light in his eyes, such a vitality in his mouth, when he was ingesting his food that a shiver rent my soul.

THE CHAIN

Every day when I went to Cuddle Pups I savoured the moment when I would greet Madame Lévis in her little office. During the seven years I spent working for her, never did she suspect who I really was, never did she know that between her and me there was that obese Christ who was eating up our lives ... Until the day when everything toppled over.

I had finished my day's work, I wasn't thinking about anything; in fact, if I was thinking about something, I was wondering if I were happy. I told myself that I was. My life had meaning: I loved Jean, I took from him a strange calm, a kind of anaesthetic. He lived in my thoughts, I couldn't hide anything from him. My life, like an infinite road led nowhere but generated no anxiety. Yes, that may be what I was telling myself at the moment I drove through a red light – the way we move from one idea to another.

I regained consciousness in a hospital bed. I learned subsequently that a delivery truck had crashed into the side of my vehicle. The driver had not been injured. My car was a total loss. I had suffered a severe concussion and minor injuries to my shoulder. I was passive but ever since I'd come out of the coma, a sole and single thought obsessed me: I had to escape the hospital to go and look after Jean. I was in full panic mode. It was now four days that he'd been alone, chained up in his bedroom, starving and thirsty. I tried to get out of bed but it was a waste of time and effort. I lost my balance, my legs gave way under me, atrocious pain in my head made me go horizontal again. I had to accept that I must wait another day, then another, but my condition did not improve. It was sheer hell, Jean was in danger. I had no choice, I called Madame Lévis, explained quickly why I was absent from work. She offered at once to come to the hospital. I stopped, there was something more important to do: go home without delay to take care of my dog.

I couldn't find any other way to encourage the woman to look for her child, to save him when she thought he'd been dead for years. If I had told her the truth she'd have said I was insane, she'd have understood nothing. Time was short. Telling her a dog was dying of thirst at my house, tied up to a chain, I knew that she'd rush there immediately to rescue it. She just had to go in the back door. A key was hidden under a flower box, she'd find it easily.

I hung up and allowed my tears, held back by anxiety until then, to flow. What else could I have done to save Jean? Who else could I have called? She would recognize her son despite his long beard and his obesity. She would pity him, would understand his suffering, would realize finally that he was innocent. She would share our secret. I lost consciousness before finishing the Our Father that I'd started in the hope that everything would happen just as I'd imagined it would.

I left the hospital four days later, against the advice of the doctor who wanted to keep me under observation. I had recovered physically, taking a few steps without losing my balance or feeling overcome with nausea. An indescribable torment, though, wrenched my heart:

I'd heard nothing from Madame Lévis since my phone call. I'd tried unsuccessfully to reach her on her cell. I comforted myself by justifying her silence as bewilderment at having found her son. She was in shock and needed time before she could talk about it. Then, I imagined the worst: she had come too late, finding a cold corpse. Delirious as I was, none of those scenarios was viable for very long, and others took over. Madame Lévis didn't call me because she suspected me of kidnapping her son. Or, still thinking him guilty, she'd had him poisoned. The house was searched, the body of Josiane Gravel had been found in the cellar. Any minute now, police would burst into my hospital room and worm a confession out of me.

Or else Jean had regained the power of speech in his mother's presence, had explained about being attacked in the cemetery, my devotion to him, my love, all would be for the best in the best of all possible worlds ... I was becoming confused, I felt delirious, moving in a few minutes from the cruellest distress to the vainest euphoria.

At the outset I had not allowed myself to call Cuddle Pups, afraid to involve Madame Bellavance in this business. But I was nearly at the breaking point on the eve of my discharge so I ventured a call and heard a recorded message informing clients that the services offered by Cuddle Pups would be unavailable for an unspecified length of time. Something had gone wrong.

In the taxi home I shivered with cold. Yet it was a warm and sunny summer day. I asked the driver to close the car windows. I watched people on the street. They were brimming with happiness, you'd think they were in a film about how wonderful life is or that they'd agreed to plot against me by letting me know with their smiles and lighthearted gait that I was not part of their carefree world of light.

The taxi gone, I stayed for a long moment on the doorstep, fear in my belly. I entered, listened carefully, glanced quickly around me. Everything seemed normal and that, oddly, increased my anxiety. I went upstairs, pressed my ear against the door to his room: I heard absolutely nothing. I was now convinced that Jean was dead and Madame Lévis had not come. I half-opened the door, the room was flooded with sunlight. I took a step inside, blinded. His body rested on the bed. He seemed enormous, bathed in the overabundance of light. He was beautiful, perfect, intact. Death had not corrupted his body. I thought about my mother and about the beatified woman who had so impressed her in Rome. I too was entitled to a miracle. As I approached I noticed that he didn't have his chain. At the very moment when that detail struck me, Jean opened his eyes and looked at me. I understood at once that something appalling had happened.

I sped downstairs and out the back door. The key was no longer under the flower box. I ran to the kitchen, opened a cupboard, there was no food left on the shelves. I rummaged in the garbage can by the sink, found a pile of empty cans. Opening the fridge I could no longer lie to myself, I knew what was waiting for me, I had *seen* it in Jean's eyes just now.

The fridge was empty. The only thing left was a small plate on which, amazingly intense, sparkled the green iris of an eye.

I hurried to the cellar. The body of Madame Lévis lay on top of the garbage bags that held my mother's belongings. I pushed the bags aside, dug in the same place as years earlier, threw the mutilated body of Madame Lévis on top of the decomposing body of Josiane Gravel. It took me a long time, I was weak, my shoulder was torturing me, and after each thrust of the shovel I had to catch my breath. When I came back up from the cellar, Jean was waiting for me in the kitchen. He was hungry. Stunned, body soaked in sweat, I went out to buy some food.

The eye stayed in the fridge a few days. Then I flushed it down the toilet. Watching it disappear in the swirl of water, I felt that at the same time I had just discarded my own soul. If there existed a secret place in every person, a sacred place unattainable by others, Jean had taken possession of mine, had planted his cross there. I had no will of my own; henceforth Jean and I formed a single person but it was he who gave the orders. I received them without his having to say a single word and I put all my energy into obeying them. Following my return, instead of battering him to death, I cared for him as usual, not hating him, not feeling ashamed, not ceasing to love him. I fed him whatever and whenever he wanted. I cut his hair and his beard, shaved his head. I surprised myself recognizing in that Christ of flesh, in the bare and bloated face, the evil I had introduced into the house, fed and protected, the evil I had mistaken for suffering. My blindness about him now seemed incomprehensible. Jean was guilty of everything he was accused of. Reflected in his green eyes and trembling like a flame was the vision of other crimes he had committed.

Corporal Alex Lévis had had a long career in rape and murder. Émilie Langevin hadn't been the only one. Other women had perished by his hand, brutally mutilated. I realized that in a cold stupor. At times my memories wavered, I could no longer tell if it was Jean or me who had stabbed Josiane Gravel with a knife, Jean or me who had killed his mother.

Thy will be done …

The disappearance of Madame Lévis had created a media storm. After the son, it was the mother's turn to disappear without a trace. The police investigation came to nothing. Madame Bellavance had taken over the business after closing it briefly. The after-effects of my concussion faded, leaving me in spite of everything, subject to recurrent headaches. I went back to work at Cuddle Pups a few weeks after my accident. It was harder than before, there were just two of us to do all the work. Madame Bellavance had lost her usual confidence and counted on me more and more for support.

Give us this day our daily bread …

My hours of work increased though my meagre salary did not. I had a lot of trouble balancing my budget. Every day, Jean's voraciousness took on proportions that were way out of the ordinary. There were now no limits to his piggishness. If he wasn't sleeping he was eating. I brought home astronomical quantities of frozen food, fries in particular, that Jean shovelled in by the package full. My free time was devoted to buying and preparing food. To save money I bought everything in bulk: frozen chickens, whole quarters of beef, jars of jam and cartons of molasses, stockpiles of frozen pizzas and hamburgers, eggs in the hundreds, crates of bananas … Several vendors thought I was supplying a restaurant. In a few years Jean put on an impressive mass of fat. His obesity fascinated me, as if it freed him from humanity. His legs became so voluminous they were always splayed like those of a frog. The fat swallowed his neck, his forearms. His sex was no longer visible, buried in a magma of folds. He no longer got up, he'd become too heavy. I reinforced his bed, which risked collapsing, put in a system of pulleys to lift part of his body, which allowed me to wash him properly. I earlier had abdicated my commitment to avoiding bedsores, he was covered with them. Some parts of his body even seemed necrotic. Jean no longer lived in the room, he *was* the room. To get him out of the house we'd have had to fell the oak in front, destroy the window and part of the wall, rent a crane. I had become a foster mother, a prisoner of her monstrous child.

Forgive us our trespasses …

My mother had wanted to kill me, she should have done it. Madame Lévis had carried in her womb a fatal foetus, she should have thrown it down the toilet. Our births weren't worth the death of a dog.

As we forgive those who trespass against us …

One day I caught Madame Bellavance in tears. When she saw me she threw herself into my arms. For a moment I didn't know how to behave. Finally I understood that she wanted me to comfort her. I held her against me so awkwardly that she freed herself abruptly. To clear up the discomfort that had settled in I asked what was wrong. She confided that her business was heading for disaster unless she did something to improve the service. The clientele was shrinking, the competition expanding non-stop. The ventilation system had slowed down, the permanent odour in the premises was repellent. The outdated pipes needed replacing, the whole place needed painting, renovating. She didn't have the money to pay for the repairs. And besides she was feeling lonely since her divorce. Her daughter was married and now lived abroad with her husband. The disappearance of Madame Lévis had disturbed her. Life frightened her. She had no one but me.

The following day Madame Bellavance proposed that I join forces with her. I could apply for a loan, I could mortgage my house. The renovations could begin right away. Soon everything would be better. She valued me very much, trusted me. I was a serious man, strict, kind, amiable. An unobtrusive man, a secretive man. We could become closer, know one another better. Beyond our devotion to dogs what did we know about each other? She had no idea whom she was dealing with. I would be her saviour. Unfortunately for her.

Our father who art in heaven ... Deliver us from evil ...

That prayer was just a bad joke. I could no longer be delivered.

Too late.

PHOTO: Valérie Jodoin Keaton

A three-time Governor General's Award winner, Order of Canada member, and *chevalier de l'Ordre national du Québec*, Sheila Fischman has translated from French to English more than one hundred novels by prominent Quebec writers such as Michel Tremblay, Jacques Poulin, Anne Hébert, François Gravel, Marie-Claire Blais, Roch Carrier, and Larry Tremblay. She is a founding member of the Literary Translators' Association of Canada and has also been a book columnist for the *Globe and Mail* and the *Montreal Gazette*.

PHOTO: Bernard Préfontaine

Larry Tremblay is an author, stage director, actor, teacher, and specialist in Kathakali, an elaborate form of South Indian dance theatre. He has published more than twenty books as a novelist, poet, and essayist, and is one of Quebec's most-produced and translated playwrights (his plays have been translated into twelve languages). In 2006 he received the Canada Council Victor Martyn Lynch–Staunton Award for an outstanding body of work at mid-career. In 2008 and 2011 he was a finalist for the Siminovitch Prize.

COLOPHON

The Obese Christ's body text is 12/15 Arno Pro
set in 21 pica measures, 32 lines per page.
The sans serif title font is Hitchcock.

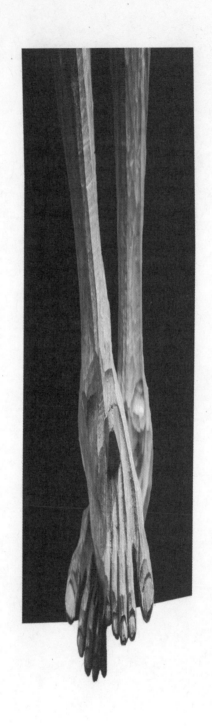